new

DUBLINERS

EDITED BY
OONA FRAWLEY

**NEW
ISLAND**

new DUBLINERS
First published 2005
by New Island
2 Brookside
Dundrum Road
Dublin 14
www.newisland.ie

'Pictures' by Desmond Hogan first appeared in *Element*, edited by Mari-Aymone
Djeribi, Leitrim: Mermaid Turbulence.

The authors have asserted their moral rights.

ISBN 1 904301 72 X

British Library Cataloguing in Publication Data. A CIP catalogue record for this book
is available from the British Library.

Typeset by New Island
Cover design by Fidelma Slattery @ New Island
Printed in the UK by CPD, Ebbw Vale, Wales

New Island received financial assistance from The Arts Council
(An Chomhairle Ealaíon), Dublin, Ireland

10 9 8 7 6 5 4 3 2 1

CONTENTS

Introduction *Oona Frawley* v

Two Little Clouds *Joseph O'Connor* 1

Recuperation *Roddy Doyle* 18

Mrs Hyde Frolics in the Eel Pit *Ivy Bannister* 30

Pictures *Desmond Hogan* 43

As if There Were Trees *Colum McCann* 53

The Assessment *Bernard MacLaverty* 61

All That Matters *Maeve Binchy* 79

Patio Nights *Anthony Glavin* 97

Martha's Streets *Dermot Bolger* 106

Benny Gets the Blame *Clare Boylan* 115

The Sunday Father *Frank McGuinness* 123

Notes on the Authors 151

INTRODUCTION

Oona Frawley

When he wrote most of the stories
that became *Dubliners* in 1904–5, Joyce
believed that no one had yet 'presented
Dublin to the world'. A century later,
Dublin has a place on the literary stage
that would no doubt have delighted
Joyce. As Ireland, Irish identity and
Irish literature have undergone so
many multifarious changes over the
century, so too, we might imagine,
have Dubliners. To mark the one
hundred years since Joyce's original
Dubliners was written, leading Irish
authors were asked to celebrate Joyce
and the Dublin of our own time. The
result is this volume. It does not allow
simply for a consideration of Joyce's
enduring influence on Irish literature;
New Dubliners also offers expansive,

imaginative, hilarious, poignant and daring considerations of the life of Joyce's much changed capital city.

Packed with caustic humour and subtle insight, these stories create portraits of Dubliners of the twenty-first century. Joseph O'Connor scrutinises Dublin from the perspective of a returned emigrant in 'Two Little Clouds', which pays tribute to Joyce's 'A Little Cloud' and Dublin characters with a hard humour and repartee that Joyce would surely have appreciated. Roddy Doyle's thoughtful 'Recuperation' forces us to consider the silences that mount within families and the ways in which Irish family life continues to change, as his retired main character walks for his health amid Dublin's new suburbs. With 'Mrs Hyde Frolics in the Eel Pit' Ivy Bannister takes a sardonic and subversive look inside the life of a well-to-do Dublin housewife whose compulsive shopping might be the tip of a family iceberg. In 'Pictures' Desmond Hogan provides a lyrical glimpse at a Dublin suburb of particular importance to Joyce's work through a narrative that swerves through time with a peculiar grace. With 'As if There Were Trees' Colum McCann reminds us that not all of contemporary Dublin has been visited by economic success, and draws a startling picture of the collision between the world of the immigrant come to Dublin and the world of the inner city and its struggles. Bernard MacLaverty traces the experiences of a Northern woman whose independence is threatened by her sliding memory and who movingly battles against 'The Assessment' of her doctors.

Maeve Binchy follows the events of a young girl's heartening discovery of 'All That Matters' as she attempts to create a new identity for herself at the urging of her glamorous New York aunt. Anthony Glavin's 'Patio Nights' offers insight into those whose suburban Dublin existence is marked by a removal from practical and physical work, but for whom the private DIY work of realisation is possible. Dermot Bolger pays homage to the spirit of Joyce in 'Martha's Streets', reminding us that Joyce would never have become 'Joyce' without dedicated readers like his inspiring title character. Clare Boylan's 'Benny Gets the Blame' captures a distinctive Dublin voice and language, taking us on a breathless chariot race modelled on a certain *Ben Hur*. And, finally, Frank McGuinness's 'The Sunday Father' follows the return of an emigrant to Dublin for the funeral of his father, who has died on the same day as Princess Diana, providing a biting, fantastical view of the new Ireland.

As a volume, these stories work to reveal the enormous changes that have occurred in Dublin and in Ireland since Joyce wrote *Dubliners*, but they also suggest continuities and connections between Joyce's time and our own. And among the many connections is one for which we should be grateful: Dubliners remain the subject matter of enormously gifted writers.

Two Little Clouds

Joseph O'Connor

A decade or more had passed since I'd seen him. But here he was, in the ample flesh, through the glinting window of a real-estate agency on Fownes Street, a hallucination in shirt-sleeves and crumpled suit trousers. Forty pounds heavier and just about bald, but it was him right enough. I almost wanted to keep walking. Holy Christ — so Ruth had been right. Eddie back in Dublin, flogging flats for a living. He grinned and mouthed my name as he clocked me through the window. But he didn't look delighted to see me.

'How's tricks?' I asked, when he came out and shook hands.

'Bleedin state of you,' he beamed. 'Victor Mature.'

Eddie was the kind of guy I used to attempt to latch onto, back in my early days in London. Hip, facetious, indifferent to convention, he'd shape into the Bunch of Grapes in his shabby denim jacket, in his tattered leather jeans and Sex Pistols T-shirt, his brothel-creeper shoes so utterly grubby it was impossible to picture them having once been clean. Saturday nights, the place would be heaving with yuppie Irish – I suppose it was a home-away-from-home. Posters of Killarney cottages and Patrick Kavanagh. Agricultural tackle hanging on the walls. A regiment of southside émigrés storming the bar. One glance from Eddie and his pint would be put up. Not even a glance – a raising of an eyebrow.

There was gossip in my crowd that he managed a band, that they'd signed to one of the majors and were about to record an album. I don't know if it was true, but he never dampened the talk. He'd just smile this studiedly unassuming grin – think Bill Clinton only with cheekbones, you're not far off – and say he couldn't go into the details. 'For contractual reasons. You know how it is.'

I don't know that I ever talked to Eddie for longer than a few minutes. He was just always *around*, chewing it with some wannabe model, slumping against the brickwork like he was propping it up. To be honest, I thought myself too uncool for him to like me. (You're twenty-one in London, you want everyone to like you.)

I'd spent two years after the Leaving Cert studying to be a Jesuit, and even after I'd jacked it in, I still felt that people saw me as a priest. They'd watch their language – infuriating stuff like that.

They'd tell me their sins when they'd had a few jars. Eddie never confessed, and that was inspirational. He'd take you on your terms. He didn't judge.

I'd see him at gigs, parties, clubs. He'd pitch up at the odd poetry reading, but he rarely stayed to the end. For a while, I was kicking around with this girl who did the London publicity for U2 and one time she got us tickets for a Dylan gig at the Hammersmith Odeon. At the backstage party afterwards, there was old Eddie: in the roped-off area for VIPs, one arm around The Edge, the other around Tom Paulin, his fag-ash being flicked into a champagne flute held by a one-time member of Bananarama. A face like a Michelangelo, someone once said of Eddie. And a neck like a jockey's bollocks.

It was rumoured around the pubs that he had an on–off girlfriend, who was said to be from small-town Donegal and not much of a rock-chick. But that didn't seem likely, and I certainly didn't ask him. He was one of those Irish males you don't ask questions: the type with an ectoplasm of elusiveness around him. Often, if you were jarred, you'd have the impression of him looking *out* at you from inside his head, through this swirling fog of ambiguity. Eddie Virago, the king of cagey, wearing his Mohican like a crown.

Now the Mohican was gone but his eyes were still bright. We stood there on Fownes Street and he pumped my hand. He hadn't heard I was back in the 'hood; if he had, he would have belled me about hooking up for a scoop. Nah, he didn't see much of the old crew any more. Too busy with the job, man. Working his langer to the bone.

'Skinny bastard,' he chuckled, jabbing me lightly in the gut. 'What's your secret? The old liposuction, is it? Course I wouldn't mind gettin it all sucked out myself. Dependin on who was doin the suckin, says you.'

It was after five by now; he was about to knock off work. So he invited me down to the Clarence for a bev. I said I was pressed for time – we'd do it again. (I'd promised to be home by six to bath the baby, but for some reason I didn't tell him that.) 'Come on for the one anyway,' he said, and he grinned. 'Let's chew the old fat. Plenty of it to chew, right?'

It was of those Dublin summer evenings that smells of fresh linen. Pale golden light was spilling into the streets and it seemed to make even the shop windows seem magical. There were couples strolling around, one or two stag parties. A punk with a guitar was singing 'Rock and Roll Suicide'. Two delighted-looking tourists were taking snapshots of a pub front. Helmut and Helga getting down with the natives. You could almost fall for Dublin on an evening like that.

He'd always been self-assured, but there was brashness in his talk now. Oh yeah, the old property biz was treating him grand. Dublin was *lousy* with heads wanting to get on the ladder. It was gone completely mad. It was *losing the plot*. Like London in the eighties, but even more of a head-wreck. Guy with a line in bullshit could rake in a few sovs. 'And you know me,' he said. 'I speak bullshit fluently.'

We turned down towards the quays, to where his car was parked. He wanted to feed the meter. ('Wankers, these wardens. They'd clamp the fuckin popemobile.') And I suspect he also wanted me to see the car. It was an 04 BMW, metallic black, with a Bob-the-Builder sunguard on the back left-hand window. Yeah, he was a dad now, he quietly laughed. A boy and a child. 'Kurt and Courtney.'

He took a photo from his wallet and showed me the kids. They were happy looking toddlers, strong and pink. Lucas and Emma were their actual names. A beautiful dark-eyed woman was dandling them on her lap. She was smooth and cool, wearing sunglasses and sipping a Perrier. I knew her to see. Audrey Harrington. She'd worked back in London as a sub on a current affairs magazine. The picture had been taken in some place like Glendalough – you could see a round tower and ancient gravestones.

He started showing me various gadgets on the car, but I was thinking about his children – the strangeness of that. Eddie Virago was somebody's *father*. It was like being told the Queen Mother was secretly a trannie. I said I hadn't even heard he was married. 'I'm not right now, to be honest,' he said. 'Didn't work out. We're still good buds.' He shrugged and glanced away. 'I don't talk about it much. Shit happens, that's all. It's probably for the best.' He stuffed the coins in the meter and pucked me a little too hard on the shoulder. 'So it's you and me tonight, Homes. Just like London times. Young, free and single and out on the razz.' He locked the car with one of those beeping remote controls and we hiked off again in the direction of the Clarence.

'So anyways,' he goes. 'How's tricks with yourself? Ever see that mott – what's her name? Ruth O'Donnell? She was one of your posse, wasn't she?

Awful looking minger. And mad as a snake. Bit of a slapper, they always said.'

'Actually, Eddie —'

'Went through more hands than a Playboy on a building site. Gave her the rub of the relic m'self once or twice — when the beer goggles were on.'

'I'm actually — married to Ruth,' I said.

He chuckled at the idea. 'Bloody sure you are. You'd need a licence to keep that troll in the house.'

'It's true,' I said. 'We're married six years now.'

He stopped walking. 'Fuck off,' he said.

'Nearly seven,' I said.

'Fuck *off*, you fuckin bollocks. Before I bate you through that wall.' (I had forgotten how some Irishmen talk to each other.)

He was blushing so deeply, I was almost going to lie. But you can't really lie about the person you're married to. It might be bad karma or bring down some curse. So I confirmed it again — I was married to Ruth — and by now he had the grace to at least look perplexed. He started humming and hawing about some other Ruth. 'Ruth *Murphy*, I meant. Used to hang around the 100 Club. You know the one I mean. Pierced lips and a crucifix.'

Some kind of event was going on in the hotel lobby. There were press photographers and cameramen wandering through the crowd. Chinese waiters in white jackets were handing out glasses of wine. Bono and Seamus Heaney were standing near the reception desk, chatting quietly with the Tánaiste, Mary Harney. 'How's the men?' smiled Eddie as we made for the bar. 'Fine, thank you,' Mary Harney said. Her two companions looked confused.

The bar was jammed with beautiful people. He ordered two double Bushmills without asking me what I wanted, drained his glass in two long swigs and ordered another. 'So what are you at yourself?' he asked me then, and when I told him journalism he rolled his eyes and laughed. 'Still at that crack. Will you never get sense? You want to make a few sponds, man, and bleedin quick. You might hatch out a sprog one of these days, you know.'

'We already have three,' I said.

He nodded. 'My point exactly. Reproduction costs big-time. You'd wanna suit up for it.'

I thought he might at least manage to ask me about the kids, maybe enquire as to their ages or names. But instead he started into a sermon on the financial cost of parenthood, which a columnist in *The Irish Times*, so Eddie informed me, had recently calculated was half a million euro per child. 'You're not gonna rake in half-a-mill churnin' out ballsology for the papers. That's just negligent. Surprised at you, dog.'

'I suppose you're right,' I said. (For the sake of a quiet life.)

'You want to get into the property game. Money's obscene. Seriously, man – you're wastin your life. Brave new frontier just waitin on you, pal. All it takes is a couple of goolies and a mobile, you're blingin.'

A house in southside Dublin costs a couple of million yo-yos. Two per cent commission on every sale. Selling a place in Dalkey could buy the estate agent a yacht. Even a halfway decent apartment, you were talking four-fifty. 'Course, we all make our choices.' He tapped his abundant belly. 'I coulda bought Kinsealy with what I spent gettin that.'

He ordered more drinks, again without asking me. He was downing the stuff fast – way too fast for my taste. I hadn't eaten since breakfast and I was feeling edgy anyway. Being back in Dublin always makes me edgy. Another round was ordered, then another, and two more. Soon we were on pints; things started getting woozy. High-jinks were remembered, old acquaintances disparaged, albums and bands nostalgically recalled. He rarely went to a gig any more. All that sweat on the walls, pools of lager on the floor. And he found standing up for two hours an effort. 'Adorin' some muppet, like Nazis at Nuremberg.'

He was sorry if he'd been shifty on the subject of his marriage – he just found it difficult to talk about now. I said there was no problem; I hadn't meant to be nosy. 'I just find it better to let the shit go,' he explained. 'You talk and talk, it only brings it back up.'

'We won't say another word about it,' I said. 'I understand.'

'Everyone says that, but they don't,' he sighed. (I was getting the ominous feeling a confession-session loomed.) 'You don't understand till it bites you in the hole. You're yakkin and belly-achin, but where does it get you? It happened. It's over. Get used to it, yeah?'

I nodded.

'Exactly,' he went. 'That's my point. You don't want to be carryin it around for the rest of your natural. It isn't like it's the end of the bleedin world.'

He gave a bare laugh and peered into his glass. 'Mind you, the way I felt when she walked out with the kids, even the end of the world wouldn't have been the end of the world.'

A silence descended over the table. It was as though some uninvited bore had sat down between us. By now the drink had begun to get hold of him. Not that he was slurring – his eyes just looked a bit damp. He loosened his tie, unbuttoned his collar; it only occurred to me now that I had never seen him wear either.

'You look mighty,' he said. 'I'd ride you meself. So what do you reckon to the old town? Dear auld durty Dubbalin, wha'?'

I said I was surprised by how it had changed. Too right, Eddie said. He leaned in close and began to speak furtively, checking over his shoulder to make sure nobody was earwigging. He wasn't a racist or anything. No bleedin way. Hadn't he picketed the South African embassy in the bad old days? (The only problem with the ANC was they weren't social-ist *enough* for Eddie.) It was just – you know – these immigrant fellas. They were *different* somehow. Not like us bog-gallopers. Their *culture* was different, their music, their food. Nothing *wrong* with it, of course. All very colourful. But these Nigerians, for example – what could you say?

'How do you mean?'

'Well – hackin off each other's knobs for havin a ride outside of marriage? That's just not on, man, in all fairness.'

'I don't think they actually . . .'

'Shariah law, they call it,' he interrupted. 'You

don't want that crack catchin on over here, pal.
Rastas in Leitrim. Stuff like that.'

'Maybe Leitrim needs Rastas,' I said.

'So does my hole,' he answered bleakly.

A girl wandered in wearing a DROP THE
DEBT sweatshirt. She was talking into a mobile
and looking at her watch. I was beginning to regret
coming to drink with him at all. Really, I was wish-
ing I was anywhere else. You don't see someone for
twelve years, there's usually a good reason.

'So where you living?' he asked, and he glugged
at his glass.

'Westbourne Grove,' I told him. 'Up near Notting
Hill.'

He looked at me confusedly. 'I thought you were
after moving back?'

'No, we're only over for a break. Ruth's mother
isn't the Mae West. Since the da died last year.'

He nodded blearily. 'Well, you're welcome to
London. Armpit of a place anyway. Best thing I
ever did was take the old boat home.'

'London's home for us now,' I found myself
saying. 'It's been good to us both. The kids feel at
home there.'

'I dunno how you stick the kip. Fair balls to you,
man.'

'Ruth likes the theatre. I like the football.'

He said nothing.

'It's been good to us work-wise. She's lecturing now.
She's a book coming out next year. On Boucicault.'

He gave a jaded smirk. 'Whatever you're havin
yourself, I suppose.'

'We're gone fierce boring now. Real suburbanites,

I guess. Mowing the lawn and giving out yards about the neighbours.'

'And buyin the Sunday papers on a Saturday night, man.'

I laughed. 'That happens, yeah.'

'Wouldn't suit *me*, pal, tell you that for real. Been there, done that; have a nice life, good luck. Out of it like a snot from a headbanger's nose. Once bitten, twice bite – that's young Edward's motto now. I've more of the range to ride before I jam the old nads in the mincer again.'

'You never get lonely?'

'Do in me gicker. Out every night and twice on Sunday.'

Matter of fact, he was heading to a party later. At Eddie Irvine's new gaff, out in Killiney. Several Corrs would be there, so would 'Good Old Van'. Of course he knew the Corrs – he'd sold Jim a house. He'd sold a lot of houses to Irish celebrities – his company specialised in the quality end of the market – but Jim Corr was probably the soundest he'd met. Terrific guy, Jim. Unsung hero, in many ways. He'd be dandering along to Irv-the-Swerve's later. Elvis Costello would be spinning the discs. Samantha Mumba was flying in from the Apple. Yer man out of Boyzone. Maybe Colin Farrell. Good Old Van might bring his harmonica. I said it sounded like a night to remember. He winked surreptitiously. 'You peeled the right banana there.'

More drinks were ordered before I could stop him. I couldn't even get away to go to the jacks, never mind tell him I was upping to head home. My head was reeling. I was suddenly famished. The place felt lurid – I don't know: like a nightclub. I was busting for a leak but he was going off at full-steam – talking *at* me like I was interviewing him at some public event. It was the one thing he missed about London, he said: the diversity of social life in the big city. 'Man, that's a party town. I'll give you that. London's grand for a rasher and a ride. But Christ, I couldn't stick livin there.'

It was at one such London party, a reception in Soho for the launch of some documentary, that he had met and hooked up with Audrey. On their first night together they'd had sex five times. He'd been in entire relationships where that didn't happen.

'We really don't have to talk about it, Eddie,' I said.

He was up Shit Creek when she'd met him first. Broke, despondent, with nowhere to live, several failed careers and an urgent need for fillings. Evict-ed, dejected, fucking *rejected*, his beaten-up car had been repossessed ('by the devil'). His overdraft was gargantuan, his self-esteem subterranean. Some people had baggage. 'Me, I had cargo.'

'This must be hard for you talk about,' I said.

'Call that waitress over, man. I feel a tequila slammer coming on.'

They had moved back to Dublin, rented a duplex in town. It was only a short hop from Temple Bar ('twinned with Sarajevo') but the cultural quarter was not all it was cracked up to be. They used to stroll there sometimes, if stroll was the word – rather skidded or slithered or, late at night, ran. The baby came along, another a year later. But Temple Bar was not the kind of place you would take a baby. There had been talk back in London – booze-fuelled, brave talk – of the civilised evenings they would share in Temple Bar: a tranquil cappuccino, a play at the Project, a saunter around an exhibition of abstract photography. But this glittered Hooligania seemed to him a symbol of why they should never have come home. London was a kip, but an admirably large one, the kind where true happiness was not possible, but a higher quality of misery was. Dublin was turning into Disneyland with super-pubs, a Purgatory open till five in the morning.

I tried to laugh, but it came out sounding dutiful. We were drifting, I felt, into the realm of the morose. Like I said, I'd often endured drunken fessing. But this was new. This was strange. It was as though he was talking about himself in the *third-person*, spinning me lines he had learned by heart.

Eddie Virago and Audrey Harrington. It had started as the relationship for which he had yearned. It had ended as the emotional equivalent of a groin-strain. Monday nights, they watched the soap operas like a couple of zombies. Like on Tuesdays and Wednesdays and Saturdays and Sundays. On Thursdays she went to a yoga class, run by a feminist nun in a former seminary – 'Unleashing the Goddess Within: Beginners' Level' – leaving Eddie to scrub out her ashtrays and empty the nappy-bin. The nappy-bin terrified him. He had nightmares about it. How could such a tiny being produce this Croagh Patrick of shit? By the time he was finished, she was usually back home – all Goddessed up like a Pagan in leggings, and ready to get into the bath with a bottle of organic Beaujolais. He was invited to share neither bath nor

Beaujo. Some nights they did a crossword. Most nights they didn't. Every Saturday morning they sat down together to do Internet shopping on the Tesco's web site. He always forgot to remind her to buy razors. (For her legs.) And every time he forgot, she spread his balls on toast.

That was the type of girl she was: the kind who could screw your head right *off* and hop it around your duplex like a basketball. Fabulous mother — but as for volatile? It was like being married to Roy Keane in a frock. He sometimes wondered if they'd called the feeling between them 'love' in order to save a lot of trouble. 'But as I say, I don't like to talk about it much. Trying my best to get closure. Put it behind me. I hope I'm not boring you.'

'I have to go to the jacks,' I said.

In the gents, I looked at the clock on the wall. It was *ten past eight*. And I'd promised Ruth I'd be home by six. I dunked my head in the sink a few times. There was a roaring noise in my ears, like a plane taking off.

When I got back to the bar, he was flirting with some girl who was describing his shirt as 'pure knack-eragua'. I grabbed my coat and my bag of books.

'What's the crack, Horse?' he said. 'I thought we were gonna have a drink?'

'I'm really late.'

'Jaysus, these bigshot London bollixes,' he said to the girl. 'Going for a drink means going for *a* drink. Afraid of their clits they might have a good time.'

He walked me out to the lobby and embraced me warmly, as though the bar of the Clarence was his country retreat and I was a beloved cousin about to emigrate to a warzone.

'Well – keep the old faith now. And say a decade for me.'

'I will.'

'You know yourself, man – if arseholes could fly, Dublin would be an airport.'

'Yeah.'

'You look terrific,' he said. 'It's great you're so thin. I'd happily shag your brains out. But I see somebody's beaten me to it.'

He clutched at my arse and started humping my leg. Mary Harney, passing by, gave us a perturbed look.

'You should come home,' he said. 'It's a great town these days.' He gestured around himself with a magnanimous wave. 'Just think, man – *we could be doin' this every night.*'

I said I'd think it over, but I had to go now.

'Pram in the hall, huh?'

'That's it.'

'Smug bollocks. Still, we wouldn't want to keep the bosslady waiting. Keep in touch, you skinny fuckin prick.'

I left by the back door and staggered over the cobblestones, up into Dame Street and past the Olympia. It was still quite bright; the evening was hot. My temples were pounding. I was thirsty, dry-mouthed, in need of a cool shower. That bloody awful feeling of being drunk by sunlight.

Down towards Trinity. No taxis on the rank. Up into Grafton Street. My shirt was damp with sweat. A fire-eater was performing by the Molly Malone statue, spitting out globes of fat orange flame. Nearby, two refugee women were begging with babies.

And that was when I bumped into her.

Almost literally.

She was looking magnificent, smartly dressed and elegant, in a stylish black jacket and a dark green dress. Jesus Christ. It was *Audrey Harrington*. But to see her like this, so soon after talking about her — it was an aspect of Dublin life I had almost forgotten, and one I didn't miss, at least not very often.

She asked about Ruth, various old friends in London, a Sean Scully exhibition she'd been meaning to get over and see. She missed London now; with the kids it was harder to get away. Her mother said children were little rays of sunlight, but there were times it seemed to Audrey that they were little clouds too. She made a point of never missing my stuff in the *Guardian*. It was fantastic I was doing so well, it really was. Eddie was a keen reader of all my stuff, too. He loved finding a spelling mistake or a factual error. It made his Saturday. He'd be happy as a baby. He'd e-mail all our old mates to tell them what an ignoramus I was.

'I was sorry to hear the bad news,' I said.

'What news?'

'Well, y'know — about you and himself.'

She looked at me quizzically.

'Your divorce or whatever,' I said. 'That's terrible.'

Her face did something strange. 'Divorce, my arse. I'm on my way in to meet him now.'

'You're — ?'

She laughed a little uneasily. 'Yeah. We're going to a pregnancy class. For couples. He didn't tell you? I'm having bambino number three in November.'

A busker started into an old Thin Lizzy song. A

Garda who was watching him began to tap his foot. The roar in my head grew louder, deeper. I had an image of Eddie cackling like a bastard – him and Van Morrison, howling with glee.

'Oh, that,' I managed. 'Yeah, of course he told me. I must have – got confused about the other thing. Sorry.'

'Jesus Christ. That's a hell of a confusion.'

'I'm just – not used to drinking any more.'

'Are you – *okay?*' she asked. 'You look a bit weird. Do you want to get a glass of water or something?'

'I'm grand,' I told her. 'But really, I have to go.'

'Well – give us a bell when you're over again,' she said, uncertainly. 'We're in the book. Virago in Ranelagh. Come for dinner or whatever. Meet the kids. Eddie's just great with them – you won't believe it. Course, the size his tits are after going, he could breastfeed the new one.'

My mobile started to ring as I walked away, but I didn't want to answer it, so I switched it off.

The taxi-driver said the traffic was only wojus. Rush hour got longer and meaner every day. Longer in the mornings, longer in the night. What kind of country could stand for traffic like this? They were laughing at us in England. They were *breaking their holes* laughing. You wouldn't see it in *Africa*, traffic like this. Going over the northside was torture now. As for the southside – don't be talking. Luas, how are you? Port Tunnel, my hole. One of these days it would be rush hour all the time. And they said we were a civilised country.

RECUPERATION

Roddy Doyle

He walks. Every day, he walks. That was what the doctor had said. All the doctors. Plenty of exercise, they'd told him. It was the one thing he'd really understood.

—Are you a golf man, Mr Hanahoe?

—No.

—Hillwalking?

—No.

—Do you walk the dog?

—No dog.

He'd buried the dog a few years ago, in the back garden.

—We'll have to get you exercising.

—Okay.

He walks now, every day. Sundays too. He hadn't even liked the dog. He walks, the same way. Except maybe when it was a pup, and the kids were younger. Every day, the same way. The way he went the first day. Up the Malahide Road.

Hanahoe walks.

When the dog died the kids were upset, but not upset enough to go out in the rain and dig the grave. The dog had been dying for years; the kids were living most of their time outside the house. It had been up to Hanahoe.

He starts at the Artane roundabout, his back to town, facing Malahide.

He starts.

He'd have waited till it stopped raining but it didn't seem right, and it had been raining for days. So he dug in the dark. It was easy work, the ground was so wet. The spade sank nicely for him. And he dug up a rabbit. He saw it in the torchlight. A skeleton. He'd buried the rabbit years before, before the dog, after the goldfish.

It takes him ten minutes to get to the Artane roundabout but he doesn't count that. The walk starts, the exercise starts, when he's on the corner of Ardlea Road and the Malahide Road.

He had meant to tell the kids about the rabbit. He threw it back in, on top of the dog. He'd meant to tell them about it the next morning, before work and school. It was the only time they were all together in the house. But, he remembers now as he walks, he never did tell them. And he didn't throw the rabbit in. He lowered it on the spade and let it slide off, onto the dog. He forgot to tell them. He thinks he forgot. He's not sure.

There are other places he could walk. There are

plenty of places. He could get in the car and drive to St Anne's or Bull Island, or the path along the coast, or even out to Howth. But he doesn't. He's not sure why, just certain that he won't. But that's not true. He does know why, he knows exactly why. It's people. Too many people.

He got out of the habit of talking. As the kids were getting older. He put a stone slab, left over from the patio, over the dog's grave, and then remembered that there was no dog now to dig it up. There was no need for the slab. Another thing he was going to tell the kids, and didn't.

This is the stretch that Hanahoe has chosen. Starting outside the old folks' flats. Mount Dillon Court. He's never seen anyone coming out of there. Old or young – a milkman or Garda, a daughter, grandchild. No one. And that suits him. He'd stop looking if he saw anyone.

—Do you get down to the pub at all?

—No.

—The golf club?

—You asked me that the last time. No.

He used to. He went to the pub now and again. Once a week, twice. Sometimes after mass. She came too. He thought she'd liked it. He'd always thought that. A pint for him, something different for her. Gin and tonic, vodka and something, Ballygowan, Baileys. She'd never settled on one drink. And he doesn't remember ever thinking that there was anything wrong with that.

He walks past the old cottages. They're out of place there, on the dual-carriageway. He walks beside the cycle path. To the newer houses. They're on a road that runs beside the main road. They're well back and hidden, behind old hedges and trees. If people look out at him passing every day, he doesn't care and he doesn't have to. He doesn't know them, and he won't. He walks on the grass. The ground is hard. It hasn't rained in a long time.

He wears tracksuit bottoms. She bought them for him. They were in a bag at the end of the bed when he got home from the hospital. Champion Sports. Two tracksuits. A blue and a grey. He doesn't wear the tops. And he won't. He doesn't know when she moved into his daughters' bedroom; he's not sure, exactly. It was empty for a while. After the eldest girl moved out, and then her sister. And then she'd moved in, after a few months. He has trainers as well, that he got himself after he came home. The first time he went out, up to Artane Castle. There was no row or anything, when she moved into the girls' room. He doesn't think there was. He woke up one night and she wasn't there. And the next night he felt her getting out of bed. It was too hot, she said. The night after that, she said nothing. The night after, she went straight to the girls' room. A few years ago. Two, three. The trainers still look new. She never came back to their room. And he never asked why not. He's been wearing them for a month now. They still look new-white. It annoys him.

Past Chanel Road. Past the Rampaí sign. He's at the turn-off for Coolock. He looks behind, checks for cars. He's clear, he crosses. Chanel to the left, the school. The kick-boxing sign on the gate pillar. Juniors and Seniors, Mondays and Fridays. They'd nothing like that when his kids were younger. Kick-boxing. Martial arts. Skate-boarding. Nothing like that. He thinks.

Hanahoe crosses the road.

—Are you a joiner?

—What?

—Do you join? Clubs. Societies.

—No.

—No, yet, or no, never?

He doesn't answer. He shrugs.

He used to be. He thought he was. A joiner. The residents, the football. Fundraising, bringing kids to the matches. He did it. He did them all. He'd enjoyed it. Then his sons stopped playing, and he stopped going. Less people to talk to – it just happened that way. He didn't miss it at the time. He doesn't miss it now.

He passes the granite stone, 'Coolock Village' carved into it, 'Sponsored by Irish Shell Ltd, 1998'. He's behind the petrol station, the second-hand cars against the back wall. Behind the chipper and Coolock Glass. A high wall, there's nothing to see. To his right, the traffic. Too early for the rush, but it's heavy enough. He wonders what kick-boxing is like, what kick-boxing parents are like. He hasn't a clue. He's at the church now, the car-park. There's nothing on – funeral, wedding – no one there. He enjoyed the football. He liked the men who ran the club – he remembers that, he remembers saying it. There was a trip to Liverpool – the car, the ferry. Three kids in the back, another father beside him. That had been good. A good weekend. Liverpool had won. Against Ipswich or Sunderland. Some team like that.

He's doing well. He's not tired. It's hot. It might rain. Another high wall, the backs of more houses. He has to bend under branches. Southampton. A bus passes, knocks warm air against him. Liverpool beat Southampton. The bus swerves in to the stop in front of him. A woman gets off. She walks away. She's faster than him; he won't see her face. She wears trainers, like his.

He stopped going to mass. She still goes. As far as he knows. He stopped going when the kids stopped. He's coming up to the crossroads. There's one of the Africans there, selling the *Herald*. Walking between the cars at the lights. He's never seen anyone buy one. But the Africans are there, every day.

He can cross; the light is green for him. Cadbury's, down to the left. More houses, in off the road. He hated mass, the whole thing. Always did. Standing up, sitting down. Most Sundays. Or Saturday nights, when they started that. Getting it over with.

He's at the back of Cadbury's now. It's like a park. Greenhouses and all. It's like the countryside here, the little river, the trees. What it must have been like. But not in his memory. It was always like this.

It's depressing, a life laid out like that. Mass, driving the kids to football or dancing. The pint on Friday. The sex on Sunday. Pay on Thursday. The shop on Saturday. Leave the house at the same time, park in the same spot. The loyalty card. The bags. The routine. One day he knew: he hated it.

His mother worked in Cadbury's when he was a kid. Christmas and Easter. The cinema across the road. The U.C.I. He hasn't been to the pictures in years. She used to bring home Easter eggs, the ones that were out of shape, no use for the shops. He brought one into school. His lunch. King of the world that day. He can't remember the last film he went to. He's starting to sweat. Fine. That's exercise. That's what they want. He can smell the Tayto factory. It's not too bad today. Clouds gathering ahead. Getting ready. It's hot. *Michael Collins*. The last film he went to. But that's a long time ago. He's sure he's been since then. He looks across at the U.C.I. But he can't read the names of the films. Too far away. He hasn't a clue what's on, what's big. No kids at home now. He's going past the paint factory. He thinks it's a paint factory. Akzo Nobel. Berger, Sandtex, Sadolin. She doesn't go to the pictures either. He doesn't think she does. She didn't like *Michael Collins*. He did.

More country cottages. And more behind them, old lanes, warehouses. He's coming up to Woodie's. She meets her friends when she goes out. He thinks. She still tells him, sometimes. Before she goes. Tells him she's going. Who she's meeting. A gang of women she's known for years. He knows them all. He knows their husbands. They used to go out together, the men and the women. It wasn't too bad. Not now though, not in years. Maybe she goes to the pictures with them. He doubts it. She'd tell him. It's not that they never talk. She went to a play a few months back. In town. She told him. Something like that, she'd tell him. He'd tell her. It's not that bad.

He hates Woodie's. Not the shop. He sees the need – wood, paint. He opens his jacket. It's a bit too hot now. He's fine. He's grand. The heart is calm. It's not the products. It's the idea. The D.I.Y.

The people who live in the place at the weekend. Haunting the aisles. And the other shops over there. Classic Furniture. Right Price Tiles. 'Tile Your Bathroom For €299.' The pet shop's gone. The big place. He used to go there with the kids. She'd come with them. They laughed when they realised: it was a family outing. Nearer than the zoo. Ice-cream on the way home. The kids were delighted. The in- nocence. It was lovely.

He looks behind. Before he crosses. It's usually busy. Nothing coming; he doesn't have to stop. The McDonald's is new. Toymaster. P.C. Superstore. And Lidl. Only open a week. Some kind of supermarket. The car-park is fuller, packed since it opened.

He doesn't know when it changed. He doesn't know when he knew. Before she moved out of the bedroom. They stopped talking. There was nothing dramatic.

He's been living alone for years. He doesn't know what happened. There was no shouting, very little. There was no violence. No one was hit. No one played away from home. He didn't. She didn't.

There was a Christmas do. He's coming up to the Texaco station. The pub is behind it. Newtown House. Two doors, no windows. The Belcamp Inn, it used to be called – he thinks. The only place, the only time he was ever in a fight. In the days when he took his time coming home. He looks behind, crosses the turn for the industrial estate. Friday night. He knocked into a guy at the bar. Not really a fight. Just a couple of digs – he was too scared to feel them. Then too scared to leave.

That Christmas do. A young one who'd just

started in the job a few weeks before. His leg had touched hers, sitting together. He was surprised when she didn't move. A bit scared. Her leg pressed against his. Nothing sexy about it. Nice, though. The thought. Then they'd met in the corridor. Him going to the toilet, her coming back. They smiled. He stopped. She didn't. Then she did. He put his hands on her. They kissed. Rubbed each other. He was bursting, full of drink. They stopped. He went to the jacks, came back, and it never happened. That was it.

That was all. He never told anyone.

He looks. Cars coming up behind him. He waits, and crosses the station entrance. It's not as fancy as those new forecourts going up everywhere. Martina. Good-looking girl. She was young. But so was he.

That was all.

He doesn't know what happened. Or what he'd say, how he'd bring it up, after this long.

—What went wrong?

He could never say that.

—What happened?

She'd look at him. He'd have to explain. Where would he start? He hadn't a clue. And the question would announce it – the end. They'd have to admit it. And one of them would have to go.

Him.

But he's alone already. He knows the last time he spoke to someone. This morning. Getting the paper. The woman behind the counter.

—Nice day again.

—Yeah.

That was it. A nice woman. Attractive. His age. A bit younger. He's coming up to the Darndale roundabout. He never looked at women his age. Until recently. They were always too old. Not really women; ex-women. Now, though, he looks. But he doesn't. Not really. He doesn't know what he'd do if a woman spoke to him.

—Nice day again.

—Yeah.

What else could he say? He isn't interested. He's used to himself. He's fine. He's come to the roundabout. He'll go on. He isn't tired. He crosses. Darndale to the left. Rough spot. He's never been in there. He runs the last bit, trots – to the other side. He's fine.

It's dark, very quickly. Like four hours gone in a second. And cold, and it's raining. He goes on. He closes his jacket. It's bucketing. There's an inch of sudden water. He can't see far. The traffic noise has changed; it's softer, menacing.

Who's to blame? No one. It just happened. It's too late now. He can't pull them back, his wife, the kids. They have their own lives. She does; they do. Maybe grandkids will do something. If there are any. He doesn't know. He knows nothing. He feels nothing. He doesn't even feel sorry for himself. He doesn't think he does.

He's fine. He copes.

But this is stupid. It's lashing, no sign of sunlight. He's cold. His feet are wringing. He turns back. He can feel the water down his back. It annoys him, giving up, but he's – not sure – reassured, or something. He can change his mind. He's prepared to.

He makes it to the bus shelter. Across the Malahide Road. A break in the traffic. He goes through
the water. He's fine. In under the shelter. A gang of
young guys. Fuckin' this, fuckin' that. Rough kids.
Too skinny, too fat. Not really kids. One of them
pushes him. Bangs against him. An accident. No
apology. They laugh. They shove each other out
from the shelter.

He'll go. But one of them steps out, shouts. A
taxi stops. They pile in. One slips. They laugh.
They're gone.

There's one kid left there. A girl. Eight, nine —
he's not sure. White tracksuit. Mousy hair, beads in
it. She's chewing gum. His own kids were scared of
gum, when they were little. His fault — he was
always afraid of them choking. She's chewing away.
He can hear her.

The rain is dying.

She speaks.

—I'm waitin' on me mammy.

He's surprised. He says nothing, at first.

—Where is she?

—At her work, she says. Comin' home.

—On the bus?

—Yeah.

—That's nice.

—Yeah.

He puts his hand out.

—The rain's stopping.

—It was badly needed, she says.

He smiles.

—You're dead right, he says.

The ground is already steaming. He shakes water
from his jacket.

—I'll go on, he says. Will you be all right there by yourself?

—Ah yeah, she says. I'm grand.

—Good, he says. Well. Seeyeh.

—Seeyeh.

The rain is gone. It's bright again.

He walks.

Nice kid. He smiles.

Hanahoe walks home.

Mrs Hyde Frolics in the Eel Pit

Ivy Bannister

1. Carrier Bags

I never open the carrier bags right away. Leaving the goodies under wraps for a few hours prolongs the pleasure. Today I bought a feather boa. It's the colour that makes it so desirable: seagreen with tinges of copper. A verdigris green. I came across it in Nirvana's of Wicklow Street. As soon as I had it in my hands, another woman spotted it. 'Peculiar colour,' she said. Right, I thought. I could see the glint in her eyes; obviously, she wanted the boa herself. Her desire was what spurred me: I bought the boa for a hundred and fifty euro.

Michael is a good provider, I'll say that for him. Having forged his way to riches, he doesn't care what I spend, so long as I look smart. Before we were married, his prize possession was a clapped-out motorbike that he called Jennifer. On weekends, the three of us would sail up into the Wicklow mountains, and when the hills got too steep, I'd jump off and walk. And once we spent the whole night just watching the stars melt into dawn.

We don't do anything like that now.

When I came home this afternoon with my new boa, there were two messages on the answering machine. The first was from that snotty Stopford one at the school, saying that Danny had vanished sometime between CSPE and Irish. Naturally, I was filled with panic, until the second message informed me that Danny had been found, coming up the school drive with a bag of chips in his paw.

'Doesn't your son know,' Ms Stopford whined, 'that he's not allowed to leave the school grounds without permission?' That woman is a cow. But what do you expect when someone her age insists on being called Ms, when everyone knows she's a Miss? Anyway, I was upstairs stowing my carrier bag when I heard the front door slam. It was Carrie. I could tell from the dragging of her feet.

'Hello darling!' I called, taking care to inject a little sunshine into my tone of voice. No reply. Hormone attack, I thought, a suspicion that was instantly confirmed as Mademoiselle Carrie slammed her books down on the hall table.

Half-a-minute later, I heard two gargantuan thumps. 'Darling, don't throw your shoes,' I said.

'I'll throw my fucking shoes if I want to throw them,' she snarled. What's the matter with her? She used to be such a lovely child, but now the inside of her bedroom door is pock-marked with black dents. And the shoes are so ugly too. Big, vulgar black things that make her look like she has two clubbed feet.

Danny was late. I was waiting at the window by the time he came back, with a great grin on his wide-eyed face. And he looked so gorgeous in the afternoon sunlight that I don't know what I'd do without him, not at this particular point in my life. In he came, talking, as always. 'Is the cat a girl or a boy?' he demanded, a question you would think he could answer by himself at the age of thirteen. But when I said that the cat is a boy, he seemed to get angry. 'Then why did you name it Shelley?' he growled. 'Shelley is a girl's name.'

'I named it after the poet,' I explained. 'Mr Percy Bysshe Shelley. One of the great romantic poets, and I wanted to think about him every time I looked at the cat.'

'Jesus, Mother, you are so sad,' Carrie remarked, having emerged from her bunker to get herself a radish, or something else with negative calories. Then Danny joined in.

'Shelley is a dumb name,' he said. 'I am going to call the cat Stone Cold.' He whooped and war-danced, shouting, 'Hey, Stone Cold! Be a man and show us your mush!' Fortunately, the cat had the wit to lie low. Not that I've seen that much of him recently ...

'Mother,' said Carrie, as she nibbled her radish,

'you do know that the kitchen tap has been leaking for six weeks. Isn't it time that you got it fixed?'

'Yes, Carrie,' I said, 'I have called them twice already.' Carrie doesn't know when she's well off. Michael wanted to call her Jennifer. I said, 'No.' No way was my daughter, my first beautiful baby, going to be named after a motorcycle. Still I don't blame Carrie for being annoyed by the leaking tap. It bothers me too. Sometimes I think I can hear it throughout the house, although in a place this size, that's impossible.

If the high point of my day was buying the verdigris boa, the low point was dinner. I asked Danny to set the table. 'Coming,' he said. 'I'm just finishing my homework.'

'Like hell he is,' Carrie sneered. 'The retard is reading *The Lives of the Poisoners*.'

Which sent Danny off into a lengthy explanation about how the English teacher said that reading helps his schoolwork, and how it doesn't matter what he reads, so long as he reads, and that this particular book is choc-a-bloc with fascinating descriptions of people's livers turning black and then exploding. In the end, I set the table myself, which is just as well, because Danny never remembers which side the fork goes on.

When everything was ready, I summonsed them to the trough. Michael arrived first, the radio tucked under his oxter. Wordlessly, he lashed into his steak. Meat. That's what Michael likes. Steak, roast beef, chops: he doesn't care so long as it's bursting with riboflavin. Danny, on the other hand, won't touch the fruits of the cow, unless they're disguised as spag bol, pizza or something that comes with chips, although he has a distinct preference for Marks and Sparks' curry over all other edibles. And Carrie? Well, as far as I can see, Carrie doesn't want to eat at all. Indeed, when Carrie wishes to be particularly objectionable, she says, 'When you don't eat, you don't shit.' Thankfully, tonight, all she came up with was, 'I'm watching my figure.'

'Watch it while you can,' I said, 'because it's disappearing fast.'

'Mum,' Danny said, 'why don't you leave the curry in the carton that it comes in, instead of putting it on the plate?'

At which Carrie stuck out her tongue, saying, 'She'll do it! She does whatever you want. She spoils you rotten. All she is is a housewife, and she's lousy at it.'

So I looked to Michael on the grounds that he controls our daughter better than I do, only, as usual, Michael was lost in his radio.

'Does that have to be on?' I asked.

'I'm afraid so, Mrs Hyde,' he said, 'if you will serve dinner during the market report.' He did switch off as soon as it was over, then started interrogating Carrie about her Leaving, as he is determined that she read Management Science next year. 'Plenty of money in Management Science,' he said, but Carrie just stared. Why can't he see that she doesn't give a fig about Management Science?

Having wolfed his beef, Michael made his escape, with Danny hard behind him, clutching the book about exploding organs. Which left Carrie and me to linger over our plates in the warm glow of each other's company. We didn't say a word. She was thinking, no doubt, about how much she hates me, and I was thinking about how much I love her, and how I should say, *You're right Carrie, all I am is a housewife and I'm not very good at it, but I did study literature and art, and I always thought I'd do something, teach perhaps,* only of course, I said nothing because she doesn't listen to me anyway. So, in the end I was glad that I'd saved the carrier bag, because after loading the dishwasher, I went straight upstairs and took out the verdigris boa, and passed a delightful hour trying it out with different slacks and dresses, and each ensemble made me look like a different woman.

II. THE HOUSE

This house is a mystery to me. Like any older house, it is filled with strange noises, creaks and groans under the eaves. And yet, when I try to track down any single disturbance, I can't find anything. Sometimes I wander about for hours, listening and searching. For what, I don't know. Michael adores this house. It's what the estate agents call a *desirable residence* with its big rooms, high-ceilings, fireplaces and cornices, and its private labyrinth of maids' rooms, cupboards, pantries, attics. Thus were the complicated mechanics of running such a house once concealed. Nowadays, twice a week, three women blitz it with a battery of mops and machines.

This morning, Carrie refused breakfast in favour of five grapes. 'Why don't you just feed her cat food?' Danny said, scoffing her rashers.

After they'd gone to school, I counted the cash in my handbag, but I came up fifty short. My face in the mirror looked guilty. 'Don't be so careless,' I whispered. 'Haven't you heard? The Celtic Tiger has gone phut!'

The cat's dish was empty. 'Here, Shelley, Shelley, Shelley,' I called, but the scarper of little feet was not to be heard. I did find a filthy pool in the conservatory. Cat puke, possibly. I mopped it up, then drifted through the house, pausing outside the closed door of Michael's study, his office away from the office. Naughtily, I tweaked the knob.

Here, Shelley, Shelley, I thought, but the cat gives Michael and his office a wide berth. As the door creaked open, I studied my husband's unoccupied desk: its computers, phones and fax, its array of fine writing pens. On the shelves were his books about World War II. An entire shelf was devoted to Rommel, his current preoccupation. Jealously, I ran my finger over their expensive spines.

Could it be that he prefers General Rommel's company to mine?

What would he do if I left a note on his desk that read, *Do you remember when we went skinny-dipping in Wexford because we couldn't afford togs?* Instead I dumped out the box where we keep outstanding credit card slips, and rummaged through the details of my recent acquisitions. Only one slip was his. The Shelbourne Hotel, it read, with a date only a few days old. *Pease porridge hot*, I thought. He was home that night, as always. Late, but home. He must have staked a client.

I smiled. I've always said that Michael doesn't

mind what I spend on clothes, and probably he doesn't. But I don't let him know exactly how much I spend. The trick is not always using my credit card. Since I buy the groceries with cash, I simply withdraw extra funds.

Quite a lot extra actually.

Closing Michael's door carefully, I toddled downstairs to check the letter box. Inside, a solitary missive from Danny's school, signed by the head-master, but with that Stopford one's spoor all over it. *In today's challenging world, the buying and selling of illegal substances can happen within any school,* and more of the same, with a request for vigilance, and a list of the signs to look-out for.

So, there's a drugs problem in the school. Serves them right. I wasn't worried about Danny of course; he knows the difference between right and wrong. But I do wish that he wasn't so interested in that wrestling on TV. He claims that all the guys in his class watch, and Michael encourages him. Michael thinks that wrestling is harmless, that since time began boys have been trying to kill each other. 'What goes on in today's locker rooms,' he says, 'is exactly what happened on the medieval battlefield, nothing more than males at one another's throats.'

Michael should know.

The fact is that I spend too much time thinking about Michael. It disturbs my equanimity. None-theless, I found myself standing in front of his wardrobe. I slid the door open. Inside, his suits hung precisely, distanced from one another like soldiers at attention. He keeps only half a dozen: three for summer, three for winter, with one replaced each season, and the cast-off banished to Oxfam. How long will it take before Michael thinks of changing me like he changes his suit?

I banged the door closed. Its glass shivered. 'Here Shelley, Shelley,' I cried. How I longed for the cat, to sit talking to him, stroking him as he purred on my lap. So affectionate a creature, so unlike a normal cat. But where was he? All I could hear was the dripping tap.

I snatched up the phone. For the third time I rang the plumbers. For once I kicked up an almighty fuss. 'Three times,' I yelled, 'three times, you have promised to fix my tap!' Much abashed, the lady swore she would send someone this afternoon.

Then I began to try on my shoes. Thank God for my shoes; they are such a consolation. Since fashionable, feminine shoes tend to hurt my feet, I manage by buying loads, and changing them several times a day. For when I spread the hurt around, it is less unbearable. And glamorous shoes really do look marvellous.

First I put on the black pumps with the diamanté heels, then my pastel snakeskins, then the white-kid slingbacks. In front of the mirror, I twisted and twirled. Then I looked for my prize shoes, the best pair, my Manolo's, an extravagance that Michael insisted upon. He expects me to wear them when I'm meeting his special clients, when he needs me to look drop-dead glamorous. In fact, the occasion has yet to arise, but in the meantime, I've had my fun with them. They gleam, black satin, studded with seed pearls, backless except for the gold chain that loops the ankle. But search as I might, I could not find them.

The cash, the cat, my Manolo's? Am I losing my mind?

III. ALL IS REVEALED

Early evening. The plumber never came. I walked past the bathroom, where Carrie was locked inside, painting her face. She has taken to using tons of make-up. To my mind, it's like coating a blossom with plastic, but I keep my mouth shut. The sky looked black. I climbed the stairs, not bothering with the light. I sat in our bedroom, listening. *Plop, plop, plop.* Definitely the tap. Even as I listened, the volume grew louder.

At dinner, the mystery of the missing Manuelos was solved.

'Has anyone seen my Manolo's?' I asked.

'In my room,' Carrie volunteered.

I found the box on her bed. Inside, the gleaming shoes were caked with mud. A thread of pearls dangled. The leather gaped, stretched by her feet, which are bigger than mine. I stared. Why had she worn my shoes? They were hardly her style, not with her preference for the club-foot look. Then the penny dropped: the make-up, the feminine shoes, the concern for her waistline. Carrie had a boyfriend! I smiled ruefully. I looked at my Manolo's, but how could I be cross? Not with my firstborn, not with my only daughter. The shoes could be replaced. And a boyfriend? There was something sweet about the idea of Carrie with a boyfriend.

I was carrying some new sheets – a dozen, with matching pillowcases – up the stairs when I heard the voices in the study. Carrie's and Michael's. Hissing at one another. Like snakes. I stopped, tilted my head, made out the drift: something about money. She wanted more; he wasn't stumping up.

Suddenly Carrie's voice rang out clearly. 'If you don't give me what I want, I'll blow the whistle.' Then the door exploded open, and Carrie flew out, thundering downstairs into me. And there we were, together on the stairs, scrabbling to pick ourselves and the sheets up.

'Carrie,' I said suddenly, 'you do not have to do everything your father wants.'

'Why, that's very interesting, Mum.' Her eyes stared, a child's eyes. Clearly she expected me to say more.

I love you, I wanted to say, but I didn't dare. So I said instead, 'You don't have to read Management Science. No matter how much he wants you to. Make your own choices. Study whatever you like.'

Her face changed then, twisting into a frowning leer, as she flung the sheets back onto the stairs. 'Don't try that stupid mother–daughter routine with me. You are absolutely hopeless.'

But I persisted. 'So what would you like to do instead?' I asked brightly.

At which my beloved daughter burst into hysterical laughter.

'Become a high-class hooker,' she said. 'What else?' And off she went.

I put away the sheets, and when my trembling stopped, I listened to the tap, so loud now that the whole house shook. Then I decided that enough was enough, and that I was going to do something if it killed me. So I went into the garage and got the wrench.

IV. THE MORNING AFTER

Saturday morning. I found Shelley. He was in the hot press, squashed against one of the pipes, as if he had been trying to keep warm. Poor thing. His face was a hideous grimace, and you could see his teeth. I lifted him out and showed him to Michael.

'Looks like poison,' Michael said.

'Who would poison a defenceless cat?'

'Who indeed? I had better take it out of your hands, Mrs Hyde.'

Michael buried the cat underneath the eucalyptus tree. Although my heart was in ribbons, I tried to slip Carrie a few euro. Two hundred actually.

'What's this for?' she demanded.

'Whatever you like. I thought you needed some money.'

'Keep it yourself,' she snarled, 'so you can blow it on more clothes that you're never going to wear.'

I burst into tears. Fortunately, Danny — without whom I would be lost at this particular point in my life — came to my rescue.

'Can't you see that Mummy feels bad about her kitty cat with its liver gone black and exploded?' he said stoutly. Then he ushered me into the warm kitchen, where he sat, cuddled up on my lap, trying to console me.

And something else went right too. I did manage to fix the tap. It was only the washer. It took me ages, but the instructions in the D.I.Y.

manual were clear enough. Perhaps it's more a functional than an expert repair, but I hope it will hold for a little while longer.

PICTURES

Desmond Hogan

My father and I were looking at Veronese's *Saints Philip and James the Less* in the National Gallery in Dublin one summer's day, when the curator approached us in a gameplumage tweed jacket and started explaining it to us.

The curator was from a part of the Shannon estuary where learned-looking goats ran wild and where bogland printed itself on sand. He'd been an officer in the Royal Field Artillary during the First World War, had twice been wounded at the Battle of the Somme, in which men who gathered by the Lazy Wall in the Square in our town had fought.

The curator was renowned for his clothes.

Women would go to a church in

Dublin to see him walking to Holy Communion in glen tweed suits, houndstooth cheviot jackets, rosewood flannel trousers, enlarge check trousers, Edelweiss jerseys, Boivin, batiste, taffeta shirts, black and tan shoes, button Oxford shoes.

A seated Saint Philip in a pearl-grey robe, sandals with diamond openwork, clutched a book as if he was afraid the contents might vanish, another book at his feet. Saint James the Less in a prawn-pink robe, a melon cloak tucked into his belt, had a pepper and salt beard, carried a cross and was talking to an angel with spun-gold hair descending upon them both, perhaps asking the angel to help them save the contents of the books.

My father told the curator how I'd won first prize in a national art competition that spring.

I'd won it for a painting inspired by an episode of *Lives of the Caesars* on radio which showed Julius Caesar, during a night battle off Alexandria, fireballs in the air, having jumped off a rowboat, swimming to the Caesarean ship, documents in his raised left hand, burgundy cloak clenched in his teeth, to keep this trophy from the Egyptians.

I'd been presented the prize in a Dublin hotel by a minister's wife with a pitchfork beehive, a tawny fur on her shoulders which looked like bob-cat fur.

The hotel, I later learned, was one where young rugby players from the country spent weekends because the chambermaids had a loose reputation and they had hopes of sleeping with them.

My mother, usually silent, on the train back West, in a wisteria-blue turban hat with two flared wings at the back she'd had on for the day, spoke of the weeks after my birth when it snowed heavily and she used to walk me, past the gaunt workhouse, to the Ash Tree. A beloved sister died and the Christmas cakes were wrapped up and not eaten until the Galway Races at the end of July, when they were found to have retained their freshness.

After we left the gallery my father and I took the bus, past swan-neck lamp-posts, to the sea.

In a little shop my father bought American hardgums for himself and jelly crocodiles for me.

We walked past houses covered in Australian vine, with pineapple broom hedges, to the sea at the Forty Foot.

In winter, when I was off school, sometimes I accompanied my father on his half day to Galway. We'd have tea and fancies in Lydon's Tea House with its lozenge floor mosaic at the door and afterwards go to Salthill where we'd watch a whole convent of nuns who swam in winter in black togs and black caps.

I was spending a few days now in Dublin with my father. The previous summer I'd gone by myself to stay with an aunt and uncle in County Limerick for my holidays.

I arrived at Limerick bus station, a stand beside it of *Ireland's Own*, where I read of the Limerick tenor Joseph O'Mara and of the stigmatic Marie Julie Jaheny and of Russian cakes – almond essence, sugar syrup, chocolate.

In my aunt and uncle's village there was a Pompeian red cinema called the Melody. Outside it a picture of Steve Reeves in his bathing togs, standing in hubris, his chest mushrooming from his waist. In the film, which I saw while there, a prostrate Sylva Koscina, with a frizzed top, a racoon top, a racoon tail of hair by her face, clutches Steve Reeves' foot, who, as Hercules, is about to leave on an inexorable journey. The audience stamped its feet while reels were being changed. Boys, some of whom were reputed to have been in Cork Jail, on the steps outside during the day, spoke with Montana accents like Steve Reeves.

My uncle was a Garda sergeant and wore a hat big as a canopy. In the kitchen at night, a bunch of nettles behind a picture of Saint Brigid of Sweden to keep off flies, he'd tell ghost stories. Of boys who were drowned in the river and who came back. 'The river always takes someone,' he said.

On *Céilidhe House* on radio one night we heard a girl sing:

'And when King James was on the run
I packed my bags and took to sea
And around the world I'll beg my bread
Go dtiocfaidh mavourneen slán.'

My uncle told us of the Wild Geese who sailed to Europe after the Treaty of Limerick in autumn 1691 on the nearby estuary, and of how at the beginning of that century Red Hugh O'Donnell had ended O'Donnell's overlordship of Donegal by casting O'Donnell pearls into a lake on Arranmore Island.

On one of my first days there I was driven to a lake by a castle where about a dozen people with easels were painting pictures of the castle.

At the end of my holiday I was taken to a seaside resort on the mouth of the Shannon.

My uncle wore sports shoes and sports socks for the occasion. My aunt a cameo brooch which showed a poodle jump into an Edwardian lady's arms. My two older girl cousins, who'd covered the walls of my room with Beryl the Peril pictures, saddle shoes — black with white on top and then a little black again at the tip. My youngest cousin, who'd recently made her First Holy Communion, wore her Communion dress so she was a flood of Limerick lace. My aunt recalled being taken by car with my mother to the Eucharistic Congress in Dublin when Cardinal Lauri granted a partial indulgence to all who attended the big mass.

On the way we stopped at a house where a poet had lived, a mighty cedar of Lebanon on the sloping hill beside it. I'd had to learn by heart one of his poems at school, 'The Year of Sorrow — 1849'.

'Take back, O Earth, into thy breast,
The children whom thou wilt not feed.'

The poem was taught by a teacher who'd told us about the boy who ferried the Eucharist in his mouth in Ancient Rome and, John McCormack's 'My Rosary' frequently played to us on a gramophone, how when Count John McCormack returned to give a concert by the Shannon in his native Athlone no one had turned up.

On arrival in the resort, in a soda-fountain bar on the main street, we had coffee milkshakes and banana boats.

On the wall was a photograph, cut out of *Movie Story* or *Film Pictorial*, of the Olympic swimming champion Johnny Weismuller in his Tarzan costume.

Johnny Cash sang 'Forty Shades of Green' on a public loudspeaker in the town.

'It's a lovely song, the 'Forty Shades of Green',' my uncle said, 'Johnny Cash wrote it. Went around Ireland in a helicopter. The song tells you about all the counties. He saw them from a helicopter.'

Near the beach, on a windowsill, was a swan with a shell on its back, an Armada ship with sails of shells.

Women with their toes painted tulip red sat on camp stools on the beach. Young men wore ruched bathing togs. Little boys like bantam hens marched on the sea and afterwards some of them stood in naked, even priapic defiance.

'I'm so hungry I could eat a nun's backside through a convent railing,' my uncle said after a few hours so we left.

There was a bachelor festival in the town and ten bachelors from different counties were lined up on a podium. They wore black, box, knee-length jackets with velvet-lined pockets, Roman-short jackets, banner-striped shirts, cowboy Slim Jim ties, crepe-soled betel-crusher shoes. Some had slicked back Romeo hair, some Silver-Dollar crewcuts. We were told about one of the bachelors that he'd been a barber in County Longford, his business motto being 'Very little waiting', that he'd recently migrated to one of the North Eastern counties but he was missed in Longford. He had a flint quiff, flint cheekbones, an uncompromising chin like Steve Reeves. John Glenn sang 'Boys of County Armagh' on the loudspeaker.

A man with the marcel waves of another era, who had been studying the bachelors, declaimed:

'I worked hard all my life. Training greyhounds. Can't sleep at night thinking about how hard I worked. Met a girl once. She liked going to dances and all that kind of thing. I liked greyhounds and greyhound races. So we stopped seeing one another. But it was a wonderful thing, making love.'

On the way back my aunt sang 'The Last Rose of Summer' as she used to as a girl at ginger-ale parties, in a room in my grandparents' house with a picture of a Victorian girl with the word 'Solitaria' underneath it.

'Oh! Who would inhabit
This bleak world alone?'

The fields of County Limerick were covered with yellow agrimony which was said to cure skin rashes and external wounds, and yarrow which was said to cure the innards it looked like. Traveller boys called at the door selling dulse which they'd picked on the coast and dried themselves, popular with young guards because it was good for the physique.

Before I left, my aunt and uncle gave me a large biscuit which was a walnut on a biscuit base buried under marshmallow sealed with twisted and peaked chocolate, and I clutched the canary's leg in a cage.

At Limerick bus station, where I wore a sleeveless jersey with a Shetland homespun pattern and mid-calf socks, a woman in a Basque beret said to me:

'Margaret Mitchell was a very small woman but she wrote a very big book.'

The Irish Sea was Persian blue.

My father and I had a swim and afterwards a man with a malacca cane, in a linen Mark Twain suit and a Manila straw hat, who had been watching us, told us the history of the Forty Foot.

Two boys listened intently to the lesson, one with a sluttish Jean Harlow face, the other with a Neptune belly and ant legs.

The Forty Foot was called after the Forty Foot Regiment stationed in the Martello tower built during the Napoleonic Wars. Twenty Men. Forty Feet.

At the beginning of the century Oliver St Gogarty used to frequently swim between the Forty Foot and Bullock Harbour in Dalkey where monks had lived in the Middle Ages.

Oliver St Gogarty had fox blond hair then with an impertinent crescendo wave, eyebrows in askance, shoulders poised for riposte, Galwegian lips.

He was Arthur Griffith's white boy.

Arthur Griffith had founded the non-violent Sinn Féin movement in 1905 in order to set up an Irish republic. He had a brush moustache, wore wire glasses, a stand-up collar, neckcloth.

One day, in his tailored swimming costume, he decided to swim to Bullock Harbour with Oliver St Gogarty. He expired a few yards out at sea.

A few years after that visit to the Forty Foot, when my father bought me a set of art books, there was a reproduction of Titian's *Flaying of Marsyas* in one of them in which Titian depicted the death of self.

The flute player Marsyas is flayed alive, upside down, to the accompaniment of violin music, watched by a little Maltese dog and by King Midas, with ass's ears, who is Titian himself, who'd recently given the prize of gold chain to and publicly in Venice embraced Veronese, lavish with red lake like himself, as his successor. Titian – his arms still muscular in the painting, his honeyed and diamanté chest strung with a salmon-vermillion cloak – painted it with his fingers.

I thought of the story of Arthur Griffith when I got the books, that it must have been the death of some part of Arthur Griffith's self that day.

Gogarty, who'd rescued a suicide in the Liffey by knocking him out, brought the leader to shore.

In the evening my father and I stopped at a fish and chip shop near the Forty Foot. On a cyclamen, jay-blue and lemon jukebox the Everley Brothers sang 'Lonely Street'. A boy, in a blue shirt with white, sovereign polka dots, stood eating chips. On his wrist was a tattoo; the name of a place – army barracks or jail – and a date.

In the fish and chip shop I thought of a story my uncle told me as he brought me to Limerick bus station the previous year.

'They get baked jam roll and baked custard in Cork Jail. Better than they get from their mothers. One fellow was given a month and said to the judge, "That's great. I get baked jam roll and baked custard there that I don't get from my mother." "All right," said the judge, "I'll give you three."'

Later, in a room in a house in North Dublin where there was a false pigment art deco light shade with tassels, a picture of Saint Dymphna, patron saint of people with nervous disorders, my father spoke, as he was laying out a handkerchief of robin's-egg blue and rose squares as he might have laid out a Chicago tie once after a date with a Protestant girl in a tango orange dress from whose house Joseph Schmidt could often be heard on the street singing in Italian, about cycling with other young men, some with aviator hairstyles, when General O'Duffy was president of the National Athletic and Cycling Association, to swim in the Suck at Ballygar.

As if There Were Trees

Colum McCann

I was coming home from my shift at the lounge when I saw Jamie in the field. The sun was going down and there were shadows on the ground from the flats. Jamie had his baby with him. She was about three months old. She was only in her nappy and she had a soother in her mouth. They were sitting together on a horse – not Jamie's horse, he'd sold his a long time ago to one of the other youngsters in the flats. This one was a piebald and it was bending down to eat the last of the grass in the goalmouth.

Jamie was shirtless and his body was all thin. You could see the ribs in his stomach and you could see the ribs in the horse and you could see the ribs in the baby too. The horse nudged in the grass and it looked like all three of them were trying to get fed. There's nothing worse than seeing a baby hungry. She was tucked in against Jamie's stomach and he was just staring away into the distance.

The sun was going down and everywhere was getting red. There was red on the towers and there was red on the clinic and there was red on the windows of the cars that were burned out and there was red on the overpass at the end of the field. Jamie was staring at the overpass. It was only half-built, so the ramp went out and finished in mid-air. You could have stepped off it and fell forty feet.

Jamie used to work on the overpass until he got fired. They caught him with a works when he was on the job. He complained to the Residents Committee because he was the only one from the flats on the overpass but there was no go. They couldn't help him because of the junk. They wanted to but they couldn't.

That was two weeks ago. Jamie was moping around ever since. Jamie started nudging his heels into the side of the horse. He was wearing his big construction boots. You could see the heels making a dent in the side of the horse. I thought, Poor fucking thing. I was standing by the lifts and every time the doors opened there was a smell of glue came out and hit me. I was thinking about going home to my young ones who were there with my husband Tommy — Tommy looks after them since Cadbury's had the lay-offs — but something kept me at the door of the lift watching.

Jamie dug his heels deeper into the horse and

even then she didn't move. She shook her head and neighed and stayed put. Jamie's teeth were clenched and his face was tight and his eyes were bright as if they were the only things growing in him. I've seen lots of men like that in The Well. The only thing alive in them is the eyes. Jamie was kicking no end and his baby was held tight to him now and the horse gave a little bit and turned her body in the direction of the overpass.

Jamie stopped kicking. He sat and he watched and he was nodding away at his own nodding shadow for a long time, just looking at the men who were working late. There were four of them altogether. Three of them were standing on the ramp smoking cigarettes and one was on a rope beneath the ramp. The one below was swinging around on the rope. He looked like he was checking the bolts on the underside of the ramp. He had a great movement to him – I mean he would have made a great sort of jungle man or something, swinging through the trees, except of course there's no trees around here. He was just swinging through the air and pushing his feet off the columns and his shadow went all over the place. It was nice to look at really. The ropeman was skinny and dark and I thought I recognised him from The Well, but I couldn't see his face I was so far away.

A lot of the men from the overpass come into The Well for lunchtime and even at night for a few jars. Most of them are Dubs although there's a few culchies and even a couple of foreigners. We don't serve the foreigners or at least we don't serve them quickly because there's always trouble. As Tommy says, The Well has enough trouble without serving foreigners. Imagine having foreigners, says Tommy. He says there's problems enough with the locals.

Not that Jamie was ever trouble. Jamie, when he came to The Well, sat in the corner and sometimes even read a book, he was that quiet. He drank a lot of water sometimes I think I know why but I don't make judgements. We were surprised when we heard about him shooting up on the building site though. Jamie never seemed like the sort, you know. Jamie was a good young fella. He was seventeen.

I looked back at the field and all of a sudden the sun went behind the towers and the shadows got all long and the whole field went much darker. Jamie was still watching the ropeman on the overpass. The horse didn't seem to mind moving now. Jamie only tapped it with the inside of his heel and the horse got to going straight off.

She went right through the goalposts and past all the burnt-out cars and she stepped around a couple of tyres and even gave a little kick at a collie that was snapping at her legs, and then she went along the back of the clinic at the far end of the field. Jamie looked confident riding it bareback. Even though it was going very slow Jamie was holding on tight to his little girl so she wouldn't get bumped around. In the distance the ropeman was still swinging under the overpass. It was going through my head who the hell he was; I couldn't remember.

People were getting on and off the lift behind me and a couple of them stood beside me and asked, Mary, what're you looking at? I just told them I was watching the overpass go up and they said fair enough and climbed into the lift. They must have thought I was gone a bit but I wasn't. I hadn't had a drink all day even after my shift.

I was thinking, Jesus, Jamie what're you up to? He was going in rhythm with the horse, slow, going towards the overpass, the baby still clutched to him only in her nappy and maybe the soother still in her mouth; I couldn't see. There were a couple of youngsters playing football not too far from the overpass and Jamie brought the horse straight through the middle of their jumpers, which were on the ground for goalposts. One of the jumpers caught on the hoof of the horse and the goal was made bigger and the youngsters gave Jamie two fingers but he ignored them. That was where the shadows ended.

There was only a little bit of sun left but Jamie was in it now, the sun on his back and the sun on his horse and – like it was a joke – a big soft shite coming from the horse as she walked. Jamie went up to the chickenwire fence that was all around the overpass to stop vandals but the chickenwire was cut in a million places and Jamie put one hand on the horse's neck and guided her through the hole in the wire. He was gentle enough with the horse. He bent down to her back and his baby was curled up into his stomach and all three of them could have been one animal. They got through without a scrape.

That was when I saw the knife. It came out of his back pocket, one of those fold-up ones that have a button on them. The only reason I saw it was because he kept it behind his back and when he flicked the button it caught a tiny bit of light from the sun and glinted for a second. I said, Fuck, and began running out from the lifts through the car park into the field towards the overpass. Twenty smokes a day but I ran like I was fifteen years old. I could feel the burning in my chest and my throat all dry and the youngsters on the football field stopping to look at me and saying, Jaysus she must have missed the bus.

But I could see my own youngsters in Jamie, that's why I ran. I could see my young Michael and Tibby and even Orla, I could see them in Jamie. I ran, I swear I'll never run like that again, even though I was way too late. I was only at the back of the clinic when Jamie stopped the horse right beneath the ramp. I tried to give a shout but I couldn't; there was nothing in my lungs. My chest was on fire, it felt like someone stuck a hot poker down my throat. I had to lean against the wall of the clinic. I could see everything very clearly now.

Jamie had ridden the horse right underneath where the ropeman was swinging. Jamie said something to him and the ropeman nodded his head and shifted in the air a little on the rope. The ropeman looked up to his friends who were on the ramp. They gave him a little slack on the rope. The ropeman was so good in the air that he was able to reach into his pocket and pull out a packet of cigarettes as he swung. He flipped the lid on the box and negotiated the rope so he was in the air like an angel above Jamie's head. Jamie stretched out his hand for the cigarette, took it, put it in his mouth and then said something to the ropeman, maybe thanks.

The ropeman was just about to move away when the knife came and caught him on the elbow. I could see his face. It was pure surprise. He stared at his arm for the second it took the blood to leap out. Then he curled his body and he kicked at Jamie but Jamie's knife caught him on the leg. Jamie's baby was screaming now and the horse was scared and a shout came from the men up on the ramp.

That's when I knew who they were. They were the Romanians, shouting in their own language. I remembered them from The Well the day we refused them service. Tommy said they were lucky to walk, let alone drink, taking our jobs like that, fucking Romanians. They didn't say a word that day, just thanked me and walked out of The Well.

But Jesus they were screaming now and their friend was in mid-air with blood streaming from him, it was like the strangest streak of paint in the air, it was paint going upwards because his friends were dragging on the rope, bringing him up to the sky – he wasn't dead of course, but he was going upwards.

I looked away from the Romanians and at Jamie. He was calm as could be. He turned the horse around and slowly began to move away. He still had the baby in his arms and the cigarette in his mouth but he had dropped the knife and there were tears streaming from Jamie's eyes.

I leaned against the wall of the clinic and then I looked back towards the flats. There were people out in the corridors now and they were hanging over the balconies watching. They were silent. Tommy was there too with our young ones. I looked at Tommy and there was something like a smile on his face and I could tell he was there with Jamie and, in his loneliness, Tommy was crushing the Romanian's balls and he was kicking the Romanian's head in and he was rifling the Romanian's pockets and he was sending him home to his dark children with his ribs all shattered and his teeth all broken and I thought to myself that maybe I would like to see it too and that made me shiver, that made the night very cold, that made me want to hug Jamie's baby the way Jamie was hugging her too.

THE ASSESSMENT

Bernard MacLaverty

They're watching me. I'm not sure
how — but they're watching me.
Making a note of any mistakes. Even
first thing in the morning, sitting on the
bed half dressed, one leg out of my
tights. Or buttoning things up badly.
Right button, wrong buttonhole. Or
putting the wrong shoes on the wrong
feet. I don't think there's a camera or
anything, but I just can't be sure. I know
computers can do amazing things because Christopher tells me they can. It's
his work, and good work by all accounts.
He has a new car practically every time
he comes home. Or he hires a new one.
He's very good — comes home a lot —
never misses. And sends cards all the
time. Mother's day. Birthday. Christmas
and Easter. Mother's day.

The nurses ask questions all the time – quiz you about this and that, but I don't know which are the important things. Some of them are just chat but mixed in with the chat might be hard ones.

'Did you enjoy your tea, Mrs Quinn?' Any fool can answer that but, 'How long have you had those shoes?' might be a horse of a different colour. Or, 'Where did you buy that brooch?'

'It's marcasite. My son bought it for me. Look at the way it glitters.'

You wouldn't know what they could take from your answer. Before I came in here they wanted to know who the Taoiseach was and I told them I'd be more interested in finding out what the Taoiseach was. Then they realised I was from the North. Somebody out of place. I told them I took no interest in politics. My only real concern is ...

Christopher would have something sarcastic to say. 'Mother, don't be such a fool – you'll be in there to see if you can still cope living on your own. A week, two weeks at the most. They'll just keep you under observation. Surely you've heard that. She's in hospital and they're keeping her under observation.'

'Don't mock me, Christopher.'

I have every present Christopher ever bought me. I cherish them all – mostly for his thoughtfulness. I imagine him somewhere else, in some airport or city, trying to choose something I'd like. And I look after them. Dusting and rearranging. Remembering the occasion – Mother's Day or birthday, Easter and Christmas. A cut glass rabbit, Waterford tumblers, leaded crystal vases. When the sunlight hits that china cabinet it's my pride and joy. Tokens of affection. Things you can point to that say ...

I don't want to be a nuisance. That's the last thing I want to be. So I make myself useful. Looking after the old people in here. The rest of them just sit sleeping – in rows – I couldn't do that – I have to be doing.

It's such a strange thing to go to bed on the ground floor, at street level almost – although my room faces out to a courtyard at the back. All my life I've slept upstairs. Feel that somebody'll be staring in at me every morning when I open the curtains. Some gardener or janitor. Getting a peep. Giving you a fright. Maybe that's part of the watching – keeping me on the ground floor. If they find out something I'd like to be the first to know. Let me in on what ...

I don't like this room. You can't lock the door. They say no locked doors. Anybody can come in. And has.

I'm glad I like Daniel O'Donnell because they play his songs all day long. After a while you don't hear them. In the TV room all the women sit in rows and sleep – me among them. A man hairdresser comes in to do everybody's hair and if you heard him – I say a man but he has this pansy voice. But everybody likes him. There's something about him that reminds me of Christopher – the way he turns. But Christopher's voice is all right. His voice is fine.

If there was a camera I think I'd notice. But I wouldn't notice a microphone – they can hide them where you'd never find them. They could be listening. Waiting for me to talk to myself. Mutter, mutter. So I'd better not. I'll not open my cheeper for as long as I'm in here. Maybe they've got something nowadays to know what you're thinking. I wouldn't put it past them. Holy Mother of God, the thought of it. They wouldn't be able to make head nor tail of what I'm thinking ...

But they *are* watching me. Making a note of any mistakes. Half dressing myself. Or buttoning up something wrongly. Or putting the wrong shoes on the wrong feet. An old woman used to visit Mammy and the tops of her stockings fell down – like a fisherman's waders. That'll be me soon enough. A laughing stock. Nobody has enough courage nowadays to ...

There are no rules here. Just get up when you like. Eat when you like. Sleep when you like. Christopher was a terrible riser – when he came home from university in England. He'd lie till one o'clock in the day sometimes. But he passed all his exams with very high marks. First-class honours. Must have been studying in his sleep.

The problem here is I don't know what you have to do to pass. Or what will fail me. So I'm stymied. It's like going into the kitchen and saying why did I come in here. So you just drink a glass of water whether you want it or not and forget about it. Or think ...

The question is – what'll happen? If I pass I can go home and look after myself for a while longer. If I fail ...

It's like a hotel instead of a hospital – with waiters, not nurses. There's a terrible tendency in here for the men nurses to grow wee black moustaches. I hate them. Always did. I said to Christopher if you ever grow a moustache, you needn't bother coming home again. But moustaches or no moustaches they're watching me and taking note of any mistakes.

My favourite is Gerard – he has suddenly appeared in front of me – a nice open face. He's kindness itself. It's funny that – to be thinking of someone and they just appear. Sometimes I think there's more ...

'You wouldn't grow a moustache – sure you wouldn't, Gerard?'

'No chance, Mrs Quinn. I tried to grow a beard once and my mother said I was like a goat looking through a hedge.'

'Promise me you'll never do it again.'

'I promise. Now could you lift up a bit and I'll get this other leg sorted. And then we'll get the tablets into you.'

'You're very good, Gerard.'

'Once the tights are on and secured, Mrs Quinn, you can face anything or anybody.' His name is in big print pinned to the lapel of his white house-coat. He pours me some water and hands me my medication on a tray – three different-coloured capsules. I take them and swallow them down with the water. He smiles.

'Thank you. How long have I been in here, Gerard?'

'Six weeks. But doesn't time fly when you're enjoying yourself.'

'If you find anything out I'd like to be the first to know.'

Old age is something you never get better of. I

don't seem to have as many blemishes on my face as I used to. But maybe that's because my sight is failing. Like everything else. It's like on television when you find out that the head of the police is really the baddie. And you've told him everything. Where does that leave you, eh? That must be the worst feeling in the world – when you think somebody is on your side and he turns out to be on the other side. Like a penny bap in the window – you've no say in anything. What use is a bap in the window when all's said and done? Precious little . . .

Christopher must be very good at his job. It's thanks to him I'm in here. He moved heaven and earth to get me a place. They're few and far between in Dublin, so I'm told. Maybe if you refuse to answer any of the questions you'll pass. The only people who'll succeed are the ones strong enough to refuse to take part. But that's not me.

This is a strange place. The patients are all doolally except me. I'm the only one in here with any common sense. In the North it's called gumption. Down here it's in short supply.

They don't like us Northerners. From the day and hour I moved here I sensed it. It's as plain as the nose on your face. They couldn't give a damn. The Troubles – that's something that happens north of the border. Nothing to do with us.

And I hate the way they talk. Like honey dripping. Smarm and wheedle – like they can't do enough for you, like you're the greatest thing since sliced bread – and all the time they're ready to stab you if it suits them. Probably when your back's turned. It's why that wee Gerard is my favourite — he's from the North. I feel at home with him. Comes from Derry. He doesn't smarm and wheedle like the rest of them. I never could stand that Terry Wogan — I don't know what anybody sees in him. He should have stayed in the bank.

I'd never have come south if it hadn't been for Vincent. He was from Galway, a different kettle of fish entirely. But his job was here in Dublin. And I was his wife.

Yesterday I was going to the toilet and I heard knocking. There was a glass door at the end of the passage and a woman was standing on the other side of it with her hat and coat on. She had one hand flat to the window and she was rapping the glass with the ring on her other hand. Tip-tip-tip. And she was shouting but I couldn't make out what she wanted. I could see her mouth and I thought she was saying let me out. I tried the door but it wouldn't budge. There were three or four other people standing behind her, standing there like Brown's cows — queuing, as it were. So I went and got one of the nurses, the one without a moustache — and says I to him — there's people wanting out down there and I pointed. He says 'That's okay, Mrs Quinn. That's just the special unit. Take no heed of them, God love them. They're being assessed for specialist treatment.'

'I'd prefer it if you called me Cassie.'

The next time I went to the toilet they were still there, the one with her hat and coat on, tapping the glass with her ring finger. Tip-tip-tip. Sometimes in here I want to cry but crying might lose you marks. So I don't.

They've done something to my ears. The time they removed the rodent ulcer from the side of my eye – just a local anaesthetic. But in the process they did something with my ears. They've never been right since. Black and as hard as bricks. And what's more it feels like they've put them on backwards.

My name is on my door to remind me which room is mine. It's very confusing when you come into a new place like this. Corridors with doors that all look the same. Like a ship. You think you're going into your room and it's a store cupboard or a toilet. That's the kind of thing they're watching out for. But Mrs Cassie Quinn in big letters on a wee square of paper pinned to my door – that helps.

I never did a test before. An exam. Except maybe for the Catechism. You had to learn it off by heart before you could make your First Holy Communion. And that wasn't today nor yesterday. I can still mind it.

'Who made the world?'

'God made the world.'

Or Oranges Academy. To do shorthand. And typing. But it didn't really feel like an exam – you knew what you could do, give or take a word or two, before you went in. You'd be a wee bit nervous in front of your machine – maybe one or two of the keys would stick. Or you'd go deaf. Or you would suddenly freeze up. My best was seventy-five words a minute. But I'm out of the way of it now. The fingers would never cope. Two words a minute, more like. And oul Mr Carragher teaching and talking and dictating away for all he was worth with cuckoo spit at the sides of his mouth. I'm too old for tests. Or maybe I'm just too old to pass them.

The peas they gave us for dinner last night were so hard you could have fired them at the Germans.

I suppose before our First Holy Communion was a test. Fr McKeown came into our school and asked us the Penny Catechism. And woe betide you if you didn't answer up, loud and clear. Who made the world? God made the world. Very good. And who is God? You, yes you at the back. God is the creator and sovereign Lord of all things ... Everybody laughed when he asked Hugh Cuddihy what do we swallow at the altar rails when we go to Communion and he said fish. But Fr McKeown was furious. Shouting at us for not being able to tell right from wrong, silly from serious. I kept very still hoping Fr McKeown wouldn't see me, wouldn't ask me a question. But he did. You, you – him pointing at me – how many persons are there in God? Three persons, Father, the father, son and Holy Ghost. Very good. Next? I remember I couldn't stop smiling. Very good, says he. To me. Very good.

It's funny how I remember all this from long ago but nothing from this morning.

'When did your husband pass away?' Gerard asks.

'Vincent died in 1954.'

'That's forty-seven years ago.'

'As long as that? Seems like yesterday. Vincent was the best husband and father that ever there was. The only thing – he was always very demanding. But he was a joker as well.'

'In what way?'

'If we'd a fall-out he'd bring me a bunch of weeds from the front garden. Dandelions.'

Christopher said I was becoming very forgetful. Forgetting to eat. Forgetting to get up in the mornings. Forgetting to turn off a ring on the cooker and it blasting away all night. Just as well it wasn't gas, he said. All I could do was stare down at my shoes and him at the other end of the phone. Serves me right for telling him. I'd lost weight and it was nice to see he was worried about me. My next-door neighbour, Mrs Mallon, had phoned him, it seems. I was away to nothing. I wasn't eating. Wasn't looking after myself.

That's why they're watching me. Asking me all these questions. Making a note of any mistakes I make. Dressing myself like a doolally — maybe coming out of the toilet with your skirt tucked into your pants. Buttoning things up wrongly. Or putting on the wrong shoes. Looking out of place. Poor Emily McGoldrick used to visit us when she was old and the tops of her stockings fell down — like a fisherman's waders. We'd've got a clip round the ear if we'd made any remarks. Mammy was like that. Never let the side down.

I don't like this room. You can't lock the door. Anybody can come in. And did. One morning an old man in his dressing gown came in and started washing himself in my sink. I just stayed under the bedclothes. Didn't put my neb out till he'd gone. God knows what he was washing. I didn't dare look. Rummaging in his pyjama trousers and splashing and clearing his throat.

My only son, Christopher, wouldn't let me down. He's very good to me — he comes home a lot — never misses. Every November the car pulls up and he steps out of it smiling like a basket of chips. Just him — straight from the airport. Since I came in here he's taken to holding my hand like I'm his girlfriend. And he sends flowers at every turn round. I call him my only son but that's not strictly true. I had a boy before Christopher — Eugene Anthony — but he died after three days. Not a day of my life goes past without me thinking of him at some stage or other. The wee scrap. A doctor told me later that he died for the want of something very simple. A Bengal light. They discovered that years afterwards. A Bengal light could have saved him, some way or other — don't ask me how. And that only made it worse, knowing that. I knew very little at the time — I wasn't much more than a girl. Lying in the hospital with my bump like some class of a fool. A baby started crying somewhere and I said is that my baby? I hadn't a clue. Not a clue of a clue kind. Sometimes I blame myself for wee Eugene. God love him. I think I was nineteen at the time. But I was well and truly married.

'Tablets.'

'It it that time already, Gerard?'

'Your son'll soon be here.'

'What! How do you know?'

'He phoned. Last night. I told you, Cassie.'

'You did not.'

'I did.'

'Do you not think I'd remember something as important as that.'

'Here's a wee sup of water to wash them down.'

'I'd better tidy myself, if that's the case.'

Gerard opens the door and shows a man in. I swear to you I didn't know who it was.

'Christopher, what a delightful surprise.'

Aw – the hugs and kisses. He's very affectionate – kisses me on both cheeks. In front of all the others.

'How are you?'

'I'm rightly.'

'Did they not tell you I was coming?'

'I'm the last one to know anything in here. They tell me nothing.'

He likes to hold me at arm's length.

'I think you've put on some weight.'

'They're making me drink those high-protein strawberry things all the time.'

'You weren't looking after yourself at home. That's why you were down to six stone.'

He takes me for a walk in the walled garden, stopping here and there to look at what plants are beginning to bud. Christopher says, 'You're shivering.'

'It's freezing.'

'No it's not.'

'It would skin a fairy.'

'I'll have to buy you a winter coat.'

'Don't bother your head. I wouldn't get the wear out of it.'

'I'm only joking.'

'The price of things nowadays would scare a rat.'

Sometimes of late I get a bit dizzy, become a bit of a staggery Bob. I bump into him coming down a step.

'Careful.'

He takes me, not by the elbow, but by the hand.

'Your tiny hand is frozen,' he says and laughs. 'I have a meeting with the doctors now.'

'Is that my window there?'

'No, you're on the other side of the building.'

'Do you ever hear anything of that brother of mine?' Christopher looked at me as if I had two heads.

'Paul's dead.'

'Jesus mercy.' I nearly fell down again, had to hold on hard to Christopher's arm. 'When did this happen?'

'Last year.'

'Why was I not told?'

'You were. He had a severe stroke.'

'Where?'

'At his home. In Belfast. I've told you all this many times.'

'Well it's news to me. Poor Paul. We were always very great. God rest him.' And then my chin began manoeuvring and I couldn't stop myself crying. 'Poor Paul.'

'Don't upset yourself so — every time.'

I keep myself very busy in here. I don't mind helping out. When they ask me to set the tables or make up the bed I don't complain. If I see anything needing done, I do it. Makes me feel less out of place. The way some of them in here leave the wash basins! And there are other things about toilets ... it'd scunner you, some people's filthy habits. I draw the line at heavy work, like hoovering or anything like that, I'm not fit for it now, but I don't mind going round and giving my own room a bit of a dust. I was always very particular. Or straightening the flowers. The others watch television all the time. They sleep in front of the television, more like. I don't see one of them doing a hand's turn.

But what really galls me is I can't make Christopher a bite to eat when he comes. All the way from England. Not even a cup of tea. In my day I could make a Christmas dinner for ten. And a good one, at that. Holy Mother of God. And now I struggle to put on my tights.

Eugene Anthony was baptised not long after he was born – they suspected something – but they never told me. I was kept in the dark as usual. From start to finish. They've done something strange to my ears – that time they removed the rodent ulcer. My ears have never been right since. Black and as hard as the hammers of Newgate. It feels like they've put them on backwards too.

I'm sitting in the recreation room with the rest of them. They're nearly all sleeping. Chins on chests. There's a thing on the wall.

WELCOME TO EDENGROVE
TODAY IS FRIDAY
The date is 1st
The month is March
The year is 2002
The weather is cloudy
The season is winter.

Christopher has let me down. Badly. Doesn't believe in God any more. That was the worst slap in the face I've ever had – as a mother. Said it to me one night in a taxi. Talk about a bolt from the blue. After the education I put him through. What a waste. With his opera and jumping on and off planes and all the rest of it. In one of the most Catholic cities in the world. It's a far cry from the way I was reared – but it doesn't matter what you get up to if you stop practising your religion. If you turn your back on God. What shall it profit a man if he gain the whole world and so shall lose his soul. Never a truer word. But, please God, he'll come round – before it's too late. I pray for him every night. What a terrible waste.

Another terrible slap in the face was the day I had to give away my niece's baby. In a sweet shop in Newry, of all places. That was where the priest had arranged the meeting. Among the Liquorice All-Sorts and the Dolly Mixtures. And me having to hand over that wee bundle across the counter. All the more galling for me because of what happened to Eugene Anthony. The family counts at times like that. Everybody weighed in – driving and money and what have you. Of course she should never have had the child in the first place. And her not even considering getting married. I always said that. It was a sin – utterly wicked. So bad the whole thing had to be hushed up. There wasn't one of the neighbours knew a thing about it, thank God. She went to the Good Shepherd nuns for her confinement. Some place they have on the Border. It's funny that, the way it doesn't show, sometimes – the way they can hide it. If they've done wrong. Something to do with the muscles – holding it in. There might be something else ...

Maybe the best way to pass is to do nothing. That way you can't make mistakes. So just sit your ground. Take nothing under your notice. But that way they'll say there's something wrong — she's not in the same world as the rest of us. Doolally, in fact.

I see a doctor and a nurse — it was wee Gerard without the moustache — come into the recreation room. And of all things! They have Christopher with them. That doctor looks too young. His hair sticks up like a crew cut.

'Christopher — when did you arrive?'

'We'll go to your room — it's quieter — for a chat,' he says.

'My name is on the door.'

I love it when he holds my hand like I'm his girlfriend. In my room we all get settled. And right away I get a bad feeling even though Gerard folds his arms and smiles at me. There's something about the way Christopher is clearing his throat.

'Well, we've come to a decision but we want to involve you in it,' he says. 'You know how you've been losing weight and not looking after yourself. And singeing the curtains with holy candles? You could have burned the house down, and yourself with it.' I just keep shaking my head. 'For six weeks or so the doctors and nurses in here have been building up a picture of you — and it's their opinion that it would be a danger for you to go back to living alone. Even with help and support. Now as you know it's impossible for me to come home and look after you. So the best option for you is residential care.'

'I wasn't born yesterday.'

'What d'you mean?'

'That's an Old Peoples' Home.'

'It's not like that nowadays. Not like the old days ...'

'The accommodation is state of the art,' says the doctor with the crew cut.

'They have their own hairdressers and chiropodists,' says Gerard. 'Cassie's a great one for the style.'

'Believe me, I've researched this.' This time it's Christopher talking. I'm getting confused about who's saying what. I keep looking from one to the other – watching if their mouth is moving, wondering if my backwards-on ears are playing me up. 'There are people who thrive when they go into such places. They've been alone at home – isolated and lonely – and find it's great to meet new people of their own age.'

'Not if they're all doolally, like in here. Who wants company like that?'

'I'll have a look around at the various options. Choose the best place or, at least, the best place with a vacancy. But we might have to wait a while. Dr Walsh here says everywhere is full at the moment. And you can't go home. It would be dangerous – you might set up another shrine and burn the place to the ground.'

'I would not.'

'I'm only joking, Mother.' Christopher smiles and puts his hand on mine. 'But it has to be your decision. We are not *putting* you in. We're telling you what the situation is and letting you decide. The doctors are saying you'd be best in residential care.

And I think I agree with that. But the decision is yours.'

'Well, if it's for the best.' I hear the words coming out of me and they are not the words I mean to say. I go on saying things I don't mean. Why am I doing this? Why am I saying this? 'I don't want to be a nuisance. What'll we do if there's no places?'

'Not to worry, Dr Walsh says you can stay on here until we get somewhere.'

'People die,' says Gerard.

'Somewhere nice. Overlooking the sea — out at Bray. Or the north side, Howth maybe.'

'The north side — yes.'

It's dark. There's a strip of light under the door. If I turn to the wall I'll not see it. Away in the distance somebody's clacking plates. You can't lock that door. Anybody could come in. And climb into the bed. That oul man rummaging in his pyjama bottoms.

I want to be in my own house. With my own things around me. My china cabinet, my bone-handled knives and forks. The whole set's no longer there. But after so many years, what would you expect — wee Christopher digging with soup spoons. I'm like a bap gone stale in the window — I've no say. I don't want to be a nuisance. That's the last thing I want to be. I've no idea how long I've been in here. All I know is that I'd like to go home, if you wouldn't mind. Maybe my brother in Belfast could help. Paul is so methodical. Maybe — even better — if I got Christopher onto them he could sort it out — go and talk to the doctors. Convince them. And I could go home . . .

ALL THAT MATTERS

Maeve Binchy

Nessa Byrne's Aunt Elizabeth came to visit them in Chestnut Street every June for six days, and because she had high expectations they cleaned the house and tidied up the garden for weeks before her arrival. Aunt Elizabeth's bedroom was emptied of all the clutter that had built up there in the year since her last visit, and they touched up the paintwork and lined the empty drawers with clean pink paper. Nessa's mother often said with a laugh that if it hadn't been for Elizabeth's annual vacation the whole place would have been a complete tip. But then Nessa's mother had neither the time nor money to spend on house renovations. She worked long hours in a supermarket, and she supported three children without any help from her husband. Nessa never remembered her father going out to work; he had a bad back.

Even Nessa's father smartened himself up when his sister arrived from America. No sitting in his chair looking at the races on television, and he helped with the dishes too. He always seemed relieved when Elizabeth left. 'Well that passed off all right,' he would say, as if there had been some hidden danger there that none of them had expected to avoid.

During her holiday, Aunt Elizabeth would be out all day, visiting places of Culture. She would go to art exhibitions, or the Chester Beatty Library, or on a tour of some magnificent home. 'All that matters is seeing places of elegance, places with high standards,' she would tell Nessa as she trimmed and clipped the brochures to paste them into a scrapbook. Year after year, Nessa wondered who would see these scrapbooks, but it wasn't a question you would ask Aunt Elizabeth. Aunt Elizabeth worked as a paralegal, and Nessa wondered too what that was, but you never asked Aunt Elizabeth a direct question like that, either.

When Aunt Elizabeth came to visit, there was no call for jolly, happy family pictures. Certainly not at Nessa's home. And not at a picnic out on Killiney Beach or on Howth Head, when Nessa's mother would have packed hard-boiled eggs and squishy tomatoes to be eaten with doorsteps of bread. Aunt Elizabeth wouldn't want to record this no matter how much the sun had shone and how heartily they had all laughed during the day.

Only one photograph was taken. On one evening during her yearly visit Aunt Elizabeth would invite the whole family for a drink at whatever she had decided was the new smart place to go in Dublin. And it was a drink, not several: orange for the children, a red vermouth with a translucent cherry in it for Nessa's mother, a small Irish whiskey for her father and the house cocktail for Aunt Elizabeth herself. They all had to dress up for this outing and a waiter was invited to take a snap of them all blinking against an unfamiliar background of sparkling lights, mirrors, velvet curtains. Presumably when the picture was developed it too would be inserted into the scrapbook. 'All that matters,' Aunt Elizabeth would say, 'is that we are in the Right Place': Aunt Elizabeth seemed to talk in capitals a lot.

In between her visits to galleries and houses, Aunt Elizabeth often went to a big newsagent's shop in O'Connell Street with a small notebook. Nessa sometimes went with her, when Aunt Elizabeth decided that really it wasn't a good idea for a child to play on the road and wear blue jeans and see nothing of the world.

'What are you writing down?' Nessa asked once and then felt guilty and anxious: you didn't ask Aunt Elizabeth direct questions. But to her surprise, there seemed to be no problem this time.

'I'm looking through the magazines and writing down the names of people who go to art-gallery openings and first nights. It's amazing how many of the same names turn up over and over.'

Nessa was confused. Why should anyone care

about who went to what? Even if they lived here? But if they lived three thousand miles away? It was insane. Her face must have shown this because suddenly Aunt Elizabeth spoke to her seriously as if she was an adult, as if they weren't in a busy newsagent's at lunchtime but in an office having a board meeting.

'I'm going to tell you something very important so listen: I know you are only fourteen but it's never too early to know this. All that matters is the image you create of yourself. Do you understand?'

'I think so,' said Nessa doubtfully.

'Believe me, it *is* all that matters. For a start, you should call yourself your full name, Vanessa; people will have more respect for you.'

'I couldn't do that; they'd all think I was a gob-shite.'

'And you should *never* use language like that, about yourself or about anyone. If you are to amount to anything, then you must have respect for the way you appear to others.'

'Ma says that as long as you're nice to other people that's all that matters,' Nessa told her stubbornly.

'Yes, Vanessa, but look at your mother: worn out slaving in a supermarket, allowing my brother to spend her earnings as well as his dole money on drink and horses, sitting all day long in front of a television.'

'My dad is terrific.' Nessa held her head up high.

'Vanessa,' Aunt Elizabeth frowned, 'I was at school with your mother and father. I was three years older than them, but I look ten years younger. All that matters is giving a good impression of yourself to others; it's like a mirror. If you look well and people think you look well then they reflect it back at you.'

'I see.'

'So Vanessa, if you like, I can help you a little, advise you about clothes and posture and the things that matter.'

Nessa was torn. Did she accept the advice and become elegant like Aunt Elizabeth? Or did she tell her to get lost, that she was fine as she was with Ma and Da? She looked for a moment at her aunt, who must be forty-seven. She barely looked thirty. Her hair was short and smooth, and she washed it every day with a baby shampoo. She wore a smart dark-green suit which she sponged every night with lemon juice; she had a variety of smart blouses in soft colours, and one gold brooch on her lapel. Ma looked so different, never time to wash her long hair tied back in a rubber band. Ma didn't have highly polished court shoes which she stuffed with newspaper at night like her sister-in-law; she had big, broken flat shoes that were comfortable at work and on the long walk home.

Nessa's school friends had always admired her aunt. They had always said that she was lucky she had got away from Chestnut Street and done well for herself in New York. God, they said, anyone could do well in America compared to here. Aunt Elizabeth had gone away and invented herself somehow, become someone whose hair shimmered and whose clothes fitted perfectly, like no one else they knew. And Aunt Elizabeth might be able to re-invent Nessa too if she were given permission.

Nessa's gaze went out of focus as she stared at her aunt's polished nails clutching the small notepad.

'What are you thinking about, Vanessa?'

'Why did you go to America exactly?'

'To escape, Vanessa. If I had stayed living in my mother's house in Chestnut Street there would have been nothing for me here, working at a checkout till somewhere, nothing better.' Elizabeth deposited one of the magazines into its place on the rack, the gleaming smile of the model going down like the sun behind another magazine.

Nessa pushed the image of her mother at the cash register, her fingers dancing on the buttons, out of her mind. 'Some people in Chestnut Street have great jobs,' Nessa was mutinous.

'Now possibly – then no.' Her aunt was very definite.

Nessa was silent. She stared at the rows of magazines with the faces of beautiful women whose haircuts were very like Aunt Elizabeth's. Shoppers flowed around them like an island. 'Could you make me ... you know ... a bit in charge ... I don't know the exact word, but like you are?'

'Yes, Vanessa. The word is confident, by the way, and I could. But before I start I want to know if you are serious. Will you call yourself Vanessa, for example?'

'It's not important, surely?'

Aunt Elizabeth capped her pen with a click and flipped her notebook closed. 'It is in a way; it shows that you want to have style.'

'Okay then,' said Vanessa, hoping there would not be too much flak at home.

'Are you off your skull?' Da asked her when she

mentioned her new name. Her brothers fell about the place laughing.

'What do *you* think, Ma?' she asked, going out to the kitchen where her mother was peeling potatoes.

'Life is short. Whatever makes you happy,' her mother said.

'You don't really mean that Ma.'

'Jesus Christ, Nessa, or *Va*-Nessa if that's what you want. You ask me a question, I answer it, then you tell me that I don't mean it. I'll tell you what I mean. I've been sitting with an east wind coming in the doors which they leave open all day until I have a pain all down my whole left side. I've heard at the supermarket that we may all have less hours' work next month, and what will that mean to this household? Your aunt will be back shortly from some museum or other expecting finger bowls and linen napkins on the table. I don't care if you call yourself Bambi or The Hag of Beara, Vanessa, I have far too much on my mind.'

Vanessa looked down at the pile of potato peelings in the bin and the naked potatoes going brown in the air, and at that moment decided she would be a person of style. She went into the hallway and, slumped into the stairs, awaited her aunt's return. Aunt Elizabeth was going back to America tomorrow, which meant there wasn't much time for Vanessa to learn: she'd need every minute. When her aunt rapped at the door, Vanessa sprang up.

'Just let me freshen up, Vanessa,' Aunt Elizabeth said, and then invited Vanessa to come up and sit in her bedroom while she packed. Vanessa noticed that there were no gifts for anyone back in New York.

Her aunt always brought the family gifts, big art picture books that lay on the bottom of her suitcase. Things about Vermeer or Rembrandt. They would open them and politely leaf through the coloured pictures the night she arrived, then they would go on a shelf beside last year's Monet and the year before's Degas.

'Jaysus, wouldn't you think she'd give the kids something to spend,' Vanessa's father would mutter.

'Shush. Isn't it nice that she brings some sort of culture into this house.' Ma always tried to see the good side of things, but Da was having none of it.

'She's never brought anything but fights and arguments into this house. We were all perfectly happy, five of us in this house, until Lizzie started her act saying the place was shabby and common and whatever.'

'Don't call her Lizzie, she hates it.'

'It's her bloody name, and now she's started filling Nessa up with these notions as well.'

Vanessa had heard all these conversations. The houses in Chestnut Street were small, and there wasn't much you didn't hear. Aunt Elizabeth always closed the bedroom door and turned her small radio to Lyric FM.

'That's Ravel, Vanessa. All that matters is to recognise good music; you'll be surprised at how quickly it all will become familiar.'

'Is that what I should do first, Aunt Elizabeth, listen to that?' Vanessa asked doubtfully.

'Who sleeps in this room when I'm not here?'

'Eamonn does sometimes, but it's mainly a sort of store room.'

'I think you should ask to sleep here, give the place a style of your own.'

'Like bring all my own things in here, is that what you mean?' Vanessa wondered if her aunt liked the film posters, fashion articles and footballers that decorated her walls.

'Only things that are graceful and elegant, Vanessa. Only items that will speak well of you.'

Vanessa looked bewildered.

Her aunt explained: 'How are people to know what we are like, unless we send them messages, child: the way we dress, the way we speak, the way we behave? How else are people to get to know us?'

'I suppose so,' Vanessa answered politely, but chewed her lower lip. After all, you knew who you liked and who you didn't like, and it hadn't all that much to do with messages. She watched as the suitcase was neatly filled, transparent bags of underwear, scarves and T-shirts all immaculately folded on top of the scrapbooks that took the place of the art books she had brought over with her. Vanessa watched as her aunt folded the lid over the case and patted it down to make sure it would close easily. It seemed final, and made Nessa feel desperate. Aunt Elizabeth had been born in this house forty-seven years ago but look at her now. It could happen to Vanessa too. Vanessa thought of the reflection she met in the afternoons on her way out of school, her shirt torn at the collar, her skirt stained with food and pen marks.

'There's no money for new clothes or anything,' Vanessa said when she saw she was being observed. She half hoped that some financial help might be offered, but then Dad always said that Lizzie still had her confirmation money.

'So you'll have to learn to look after what clothes you *do* have, I suppose.' Her aunt was vague, as if it had nothing to do with her.

'And my hair?' Vanessa looked despairing, her fingers combing through her wind-blown pony-tail.

'Does Lillian Harris at number five still do hair? She used to be good.'

'Yes, but again, where would I get the money to pay her?'

'Do something for her instead, you know: take her mother for a walk in the wheelchair, do the shopping for Lillian one day a week; then she can give you a proper haircut every month.'

It was a possibility certainly. 'It would be easier if you were here,' Vanessa said, watching her aunt creaming her long slim hands. Ma's hands were cracked and red and had never known hand cream.

'You can write to me, Vanessa, telling me your progress.'

'And maybe come and see you in New York one day?' Vanessa was daring.

'One day maybe.'

Vanessa had heard warmer invitations in her young life, but she was not going to get moody about it: her aunt would write with advice, like someone in the papers. 'Let's go down for supper. Ma's making shepherd's pie as a treat for your last night here.'

'That's nice.' Aunt Elizabeth zipped her bag. 'But remember, don't eat any of the mashed potato on

top, Vanessa, no bread and butter, and try to en-
courage your mother to have salads in future.'

During supper Vanessa watched her mother,
father and Eamonn and Sean gobbling up the
shepherd's pie. Her mother ate hastily out of
weariness, wanting to get through dinner so that
bedtime would arrive more quickly. Her father's
fork rose steadily up and down from the plate as he
cocked an ear towards the television in the sitting
room, listening for the racing results. And her
brothers laughed with their mouths open, the
mashed potato smashed against their teeth. They
made mad faces and laughed more. Vanessa never
felt more like a traitor than that evening as she
nibbled at the meat part of the pie and halved a
tomato with her aunt. It was as if she had crossed
a line, changed sides.

In the next months, she wrote for advice three
times to Aunt Elizabeth in New York. Always she
got a frank and helpful reply. Yes indeed, Vanessa
should take a Saturday job in a restaurant, but she
must choose a smart place, and insist that they give
her a uniform to wear. An entirely fictitious ref-
erence was sent from New York to help her get such
a job. No, it would be foolish and time wasting for
Vanessa to try and learn to play the piano. She was
too old to start a musical education at fifteen; she
would be better to borrow CDs from the library
and learn to appreciate music made by others. And
yes, Vanessa would be well advised to go to any
poetry readings, book launches or cultural events
that she heard of around Dublin. She would meet a
lot of interesting people this way.

And Vanessa did meet interesting people. Including Owen, who was twenty-two and couldn't believe that Vanessa was still at school, and whom Vanessa couldn't believe wanted to spend so much time with her. She was going to write about this to her aunt, but something stopped her. Maybe it was the fact that she had never asked Owen back home to Chestnut Street. And that she didn't want to tell her aunt that, after the first month of meeting him at galleries and readings, Owen had become not just another person at galleries and readings, but Vanessa's lover.

The next summer, Aunt Elizabeth was impressed by Vanessa's bedroom, which was a cool blue and devoid of footballers' pictures. The art books Aunt Elizabeth had brought over the years were massed on a slim shelf. Vanessa had few clothes these days but those she had were ironed, mostly black and looked expensive. She was slimmer, and different somehow to last year. Her hair was short and blonde and shiny; the ponytail had vanished. 'Vanessa looks very well,' Aunt Elizabeth announced after Vanessa left for work on Saturday afternoon. Vanessa's mother confessed to her sister-in-law that the girl had become distant and secretive; her father said that Nessa was a proper pain in the arse. Eamonn and Sean said little except to hint that they were broke to the hilt.

When she wasn't working extra shifts because of being on school holidays, Vanessa brought her aunt to an open-air concert, the launch of a poetry book and an antiques exhibition. Everywhere Vanessa knew people or nodded at them; men and women twice, three times her age waved fingers and kissed her cheeks. Aunt Elizabeth was introduced again and again; Vanessa filled her aunt in afterwards about who everyone was. Once she mentioned Owen and the fact that his father was a well-known lawyer. Aunt Elizabeth came in as if on radar, but Vanessa was prepared. 'You don't tell me about your private life, you never say who loved you and you loved in return. I thought it was a bit ... I don't know ... undignified ... to talk about things like that.'

'You're learning fast, Vanessa,' said Elizabeth with a glancing look at her nearly sixteen-year-old niece.

When Elizabeth returned to New York at the end of her trip, there were more photos in her scrapbook than in previous years, many of them of Vanessa. Vanessa in a black skirt at the poetry reading, Vanessa in a black dress at the concert, Vanessa smiling next to her aunt beneath a glistening teardrop chandelier.

After her aunt had gone back to New York, Vanessa sometimes wondered what her life would be like if she hadn't known Aunt Elizabeth. Miserable, she thought. She'd never have had dreamt of meeting someone like Owen. But then three months later, Vanessa discovered that she was pregnant. She met Owen in a smart tapas bar with live guitar music and told him. He had just been saying that she had *the* most amazing taste in finding places when she gave him the news.

'Hey, Vanessa ... this is not for real,' he said.

She brushed imaginary crumbs from her black slacks and waited politely for him to say something else. Something like that it was all a bit earlier than they had hoped, but what the hell, they were always going to be together anyway. But what he said was, 'Jesus, Vanessa, I'm *so* sorry.' And suddenly she understood: this must be the kind of thing that Aunt Elizabeth had tried to escape. She smiled a cold little smile and said, yes, wasn't life really shitty, and got up and left the restaurant.

She lay in her uncluttered bedroom and by dawn she knew she would go to New York. She worked out the finances: if she sold her record player, her new shoes and her good bracelet, she would have the fare. She had a passport since her sixteenth birthday just in case Owen had invited her skiing. She would turn up at Aunt Elizabeth's and ask her what to do. She had to get away.

Her mother said that she just gave up. In the middle of the school term Nessa was going to fly to New York. The rest of the family wasn't able to go to the Isle of frigging Man but Nessa was going to New York. Her father said it was history repeating itself, just like Lizzie, gone in two minutes, and then they never saw her apart from her arriving back every year like some bloody duchess. Eamonn and Sean sat dumbfounded. Imagine that Aunt Elizabeth had sent for Nessa.

Vanessa decided not to tell her aunt until she got there, and spent the flight nervously looking out of the window at the nothingness of the sky, wondering what would happen. She didn't have Aunt Elizabeth's work address, so she got a bus from the airport to the postal address in Queens, and kept checking the numbers in the left-hand corner of one of her aunt's letters. Was this it? Aunt Elizabeth couldn't live here, surely? People passed by. No one looked at her. Vanessa sat down on the steps outside of the building, nervously pulling her bag under her legs. She should have gotten a phone number; this must be the wrong address, and what should she do? The light sank out of the sky, more people traipsed past. Vanessa dug into her bag and pulled on extra sweaters. It would have been one a.m. in Dublin. Everyone in Chestnut Street was asleep.

Vanessa struggled to her feet in relief when finally she saw her aunt walking towards the building, lit up by the streetlamps. She walked straight and tall, yet looked tired. Her face changed when she saw Vanessa by the steps.

'What happened?' she asked

'I needed some advice.'

'You could have written,' her aunt's voice was cold.

'It was too important to wait.'

'Where are you staying?' Elizabeth asked.

'I thought with you, like you stay with us when you come to Dublin.' Vanessa hoped that some spirit shone through her voice; she was deathly tired and frightened but she didn't want it known. She followed her aunt's trim figure up four flights of stairs and down a long corridor. Children were crying behind doors; cooking smells filled the building. The big room had peeling walls. An ironing board stood at the ready and a steel clothes rail held garments that would be worn to work. Two faded armchairs and a single bed in the corner looked as if nobody had ever visited them. A tiny two-ring burner and a sink formed the kitchen. Vanessa said nothing, just sat there waiting for her aunt to make coffee.

'I suppose you're pregnant,' Elizabeth said.

'Yes.'

'And he doesn't want to hear about it?'

'How do you know?' Vanessa was astounded.

'You wouldn't be here otherwise.'

'You always know what to do, Elizabeth.' Vanessa had dropped the Aunt bit. It didn't seem appropriate somehow now that she had discovered the secret life that had been lied about for so long. She remembered so many things that had been said: all that matters is to have fresh flowers; all that matters to have one piece of really good furniture polished with beeswax. Vanessa looked around her: compared to this place, Chestnut Street was like a palace. And to think that poor Ma had been scrubbing and cleaning to make things look right.

'Does anyone else know about this, Vanessa?'

'No, only Owen, and as you say he doesn't want to hear about it.'

'All that matters is that it stays that way. It's quite easy if you realise that. Now, are you having a termination or will you have it adopted?'

It was all so business-like, so authoritative, so like the old Aunt Elizabeth, that Vanessa almost forgot her strange surroundings. 'I haven't decided yet,' she said.

'Well, you must decide soon. And then we have a lot of things to consider; if it's a termination, he and his people should pay. You have no money; I have no money. If not a termination then we have to think of a cover story and a job for you. Just remember that whatever happens, you can't be allowed to ruin your life staying at home wheeling a pram up and down Chestnut Street, marking yourself out as a loser before your life has properly begun.'

It was all so clear and obvious to Elizabeth, yet it didn't seem quite so clear to Vanessa. 'It might be easier to be there than anywhere else,' she began tentatively.

'Easier than what?'

'Than asking Owen and his family to give me money, than making up some fake existence over here in America.' Vanessa looked around her and said nothing more.

'You don't like my home apparently, so why did you come here then?'

'I didn't say that; it's just very different from what you made us think.'

'I'm not responsible for what you thought.'

'Do you really have a big job as a paralegal? Was any of it true? Anything you told us about your life?'

'I work in Manhattan for a legal firm. I meet a lot of cultured people there; I go to lectures and art galleries with them. I spend what I earn in giving a good impression, a good account of myself. Now is there any other intrusive question you would like to ask, you who have turned up pregnant on my doorstep looking for help?'

'Just one more,' Vanessa said, watching her aunt's face. 'Why did you leave? Because of something like this?'

There was a long pause. Vanessa wondered whether

she would answer at all. Eventually she said, 'Yes. Twenty-nine years ago.' Elizabeth stared at the ceiling. 'He will be twenty-nine at Christmas. Imagine!'

'And where is he?' Vanessa whispered.

'On the west coast; Seattle, I believe. Of course he may have moved. He tried to find me when he was twenty but I didn't let him. I wrote and said that all that mattered now was that he forged ahead with his own life; his adoptive parents were substantial people, he had a good education. I never heard from him again.'

Outside the windows of the walk-up apartment the sound of traffic droned and police sirens wailed. Suddenly it was very clear to Vanessa: all these years of Elizabeth talking about what mattered, when all that really mattered was that she get out of this place. She had to come all this distance to realise that her mother's tired face would eventually light up at the thought of a baby in the home again, and that her father was always great at rocking a pram while he watched the runners line up at the Curragh. Eamonn and Sean would get used to it like everyone got used to everything, except possibly being abandoned twenty-nine years ago to substantial people in Seattle. Her bedroom, Aunt Elizabeth's old bedroom, would have room for two; she'd do her schoolwork downstairs at night. As the New York night hastened to its end, Nessa closed her eyes: going home again, back to Dublin, back to Chestnut Street and to herself, that was all that mattered.

PATIO NIGHTS

Anthony Glavin

A week after the new patio was laid, Sean woke to what sounded like a battle royal in the back garden below. High-pitched feral screams, unlike anything he'd ever heard. Followed by more cries and a frenzied, guttural growling. This last woke Dervla, who sat up beside him and exclaimed, 'Sweet Jesus!', her voice registering its own tiny note of terror.

'Has a fox Fogartys' cat?' said Sean, who was already at the bedroom door. Or was it Murphy that they now heard, being gutted in the garden? But Murphy was in, whining anxiously at the glass doors onto the patio as Sean entered the kitchen. Though, oddly, not barking – which as your man Holmes once observed is sometimes a clue.

Odder yet, Murphy, who always tore madly down the garden, this time only ran across the patio, then stopped and stared over at the Burkes' back garden, to where the fracas had shifted itself. Sean too had halted in the April dark, midway across the new patio, its sudden stonework cold and damp beneath his bare feet.

Tegula blocks were what Dervla had finally chosen for the patio, over cobblelock or cobblesett. Tegula, a handsome, pricey stone, available in washed-out shades of mauve, grey and terracotta 'for a nicely muted, multi-coloured effect'. The builders' provider who sold them the blocks also provided the name of a patio man, as Sean was in no ways handy for a job like that. Though he did spend a weekend knocking down the huge storage shed, as big and dirty-white as Moby Dick, which the previous owners had sited opposite the glass doors of the kitchen extension, obliterating any view of the long narrow garden that was bounded by a thick hedge either side.

A hedge through which two large, low forms now burst darkly back into view. But banking sharply left, they galloped away from Sean, down towards the new, smaller shed at the bottom of the garden. Murphy too went a few feet farther down, then turned and quickly trotted back. Clueless still, Sean moved off the patio to where the dog had first stopped, hoping for a better look. But he could see nothing past the pergola which Dervla's da had erected for them halfway down the garden. He could hear the intruders however: their cater-wauling, followed by claws scrabbling on wood, as they banked off the shed, or the wooden fence, or both.

Suddenly the pair reappeared, one in hot pursuit of the other, both now lumbering madly straight for Sean, who froze, his blood curdling, suddenly, ridiculously exposed in his T-shirt and boxer shorts. 'Oh fuck!' he whispered, like a prayer.

Only to see it answered, as the deadly duo swerved and once again hurtled through a hedge, this time into the Fogartys' back garden. 'Come on, Murph,' Sean said, turning quickly toward the house. Nor did Murphy, the same small terrier-mix who never thought twice about mixing it with a dog thrice his size, Alsation or Labrador, need any encouragement. His mama obviously having instructed him as a pup: 'Don't fuck with the badgers, Son. Especially don't fuck with badgers fucking.'

The dog hopped straight back onto its bean bag as Sean went upstairs, pausing only at the front bedroom to look in on the twins, Jenny and Jill, aged five, who had slept through the mêlée. 'Badgers,' he told Dervla, getting back into bed. 'Did you ever hear the like?'

'Never,' Dervla said. 'But my mother did, a few weeks before I was born.' Turning out the light, she told how her mother had been awakened by two badgers, chasing in and out of the churchyard across from their house up in Donegal. 'She found my grandfather dead in bed the next morning,' Dervla said. 'And she always linked those badgers with his going.'

'Like a sign?'

'Something like that,' Dervla said, making Sean

ponder what their own visitation might possibly portend, given there were no headstones outside their bedroom, only a patio.

He lay quietly then, too jazzed up to sleep from his foray outside, that moment of absolute terror when the two beasts had started towards him. Like low-slung bears, the black and white stripes on their heads just visible in the garden gloom. Lying in the dark, he thought for the first time in years of the project he had done on badgers back in National School. Mastering words like 'nocturnal' and 'omnivorous' and the Irish '*broc*', marshalling facts like the two-hundred earthworms a single adult might devour nightly, and drawing a clumsy diagram of a many-chambered sett.

Yet these two specimens, up close and personal, had seemed another species altogether. More turbocharged than ambling, and anything but cautious. He could no longer hear them courting out the bedroom window Dervla insisted they leave cracked, even in winter. But the noises they had made played on in his head – a soundtrack as primal as night itself. Sex like warfare, he thought. Eros playing at thanotos. He guessed Dervla was also still awake, given the stillness on her side of the bed, but he said nothing. Nor did it occur to him that they might make love, something they hadn't done in a while, as if he knew deep down they couldn't hope to match the spectacularly ardent frenzy that had awakened them.

Frank Fogarty next door hadn't heard the badgers at all. But he told Sean the following evening how they occasionally scattered any trash he left bagged outside his back door. 'And I've heard them other

Aprils,' Fogarty laughed over the hedge, 'having it off in your garden.' He knew a bit about badgers himself, the curved one-inch claws, how the biggest ones weighed over forty pounds, making Sean wonder had Fogarty done a school project on them too?

'What's that block called again?' he then asked Sean, adding that he was thinking of laying a patio himself. 'Tegula,' Sean said. Like pergola, he thought, though he doubted Fogarty would throw one of them up himself: pergolas being somewhat thin on the ground on Dublin's Northside, apart from in the Botanic Gardens or St Anne's Park. Nor would Fogarty likely plant the *rucola* which Dervla grew in order to ruin a good salad. '*Tegula, pergola, rucola,*' Sean rhymed inside his head. No doubt Fogarty, a builder, would lay his own tegula or cobblelock – hardly needing to hire a patio man, unlike Sean, who taught at the comprehensive school just beyond the tall trees and ample hedge-row at the bottom of their gardens. Home to the badgers and an occasional solitary fox, the small greenbelt, its trees often festooned with wood pigeons, helped to muffle the sound of traffic on the adjoining Airport road.

Sean didn't mention Fogarty's patio plans to Dervla when he went back inside. As it was, he occasionally teased her over any attention she paid to a tradesman about the house, the cup of tea she might offer the occasional plumber or electrician. Or the salad sandwich she'd made for Dan, their patio man, an admittedly handsome bloke: tall, a shock of thick brown hair, and ten or so years younger than Sean, who had just turned forty.

Dervla's fancying the handymen was a running joke between them, seeded in part by Sean's misgivings at having mastered no trade. Being one of those who can't do, he taught, both science and maths. But the one time he said something like this aloud, Dervla had just softly laughed, 'Sure, you're great with your hands, love.' And they had made love shortly after too, once they'd got the twins down.

Sean didn't mention Fogarty's patio, but he did repeat what Frank had said about the badgers visiting each spring. 'So my garden's just the local lovers' lane?' Dervla smiled. 'Is that what you're telling me?' But Sean wasn't telling her anything, not being sure himself there were anything to tell.

Two months later they were both woken by the patio itself. Or so it sounded, a loudly reverberating noise, like someone was dragging their wooden picnic table across its blocky stones. Over the past few weeks some party had been helping himself to a litre of milk from the four blue waxed cartons the milkman left every second morning. The loss wasn't much, but the sense of violation – a strange body coming though the gate and up to the front door as they slept – was palpable. 'Did the milk thief come?' the twins now asked first thing at breakfast. And now, ludicrous as it seemed, there sounded to be a 'picnic-table thief' at work as well.

But what Sean saw, upon tearing back the bedroom curtain, was something altogether else – a massive conflagration, the largest he had ever seen, somewhere on the far side of the Airport road. 'O, my God!' Dervla breathed beside him, as they stood staring at the huge orange wall of flame, its tongues of fire leaping the distant treeline and licking the black night sky. 'Holy fuck!' Sean breathed back, realising midst his own huge terror how nobody could hope to escape such an inferno. Worse yet, it felt like he and Dervla were the sole witnesses, the only other souls awake at four a.m. of a June morning on Dublin's Northside. Certainly there were no other sounds to be heard, no sirens, no traffic – just the muted howl of that holocaust, shot through with a steady string of mini-explosions, like scores of cherry bombs detonating, loud enough to have woken them from a dead sleep.

The Garda who picked up the phone at the Whitehall barracks just down the road told Sean they'd only just seen the flames themselves. 'We're trying to locate it exactly,' he added, excitedly, foregoing the authoritative reserve that guards habitually muster. Hanging up, Sean turned to find Dervla with the car keys, a mac over her night-dress. 'I woke Mam,' she whispered, her mother having come down from Donegal for a week, something she did several times a year. Pitching her tent in the box room, and utterly spoiling the twins.

They tracked the flames along Collins Ave and down Grace Park Road, where they saw the spinning red lights of the fire brigade already there. Pulling the Fiat up onto the footpath opposite, Sean puzzled at how few people had gathered across from the Convent behind its high stone wall, given that the fire had awakened him and Dervla a half-mile away as the crow flies. As they stood gaping at the flame-engulfed, three-storey stone building, one of the near neighbours, an older man in a pullover, told Sean how nobody slept there any longer. 'It's the timber in the roof you heard,' he said, 'the pockets of pitch pine exploding.' Speaking with a quiet authority, that of a carpenter or roofer.

They stood for a few minutes more, watching the fire tenders hurl their water up at the building, like white ropes in the night, before they turned away. 'I think that's where the Magdalen girls used to live,' Dervla said driving home, making Sean think of recent revelations of abuse by the religious of those in their care in such buildings down the decades. Of how there had been fates arguably worse than death meted out – often by teachers like himself – to orphans, unmarried mothers or children taken from their families throughout Ireland. Yet try as he might, he could not shift the feeling that had followed his drawing back the curtain a half-hour before – to gaze out onto what had looked, and sounded, utterly implacable, inevitable, beyond propitiation.

Nor did the tiny white stars scattered across the black sky over their front garden offer much comfort, as Dervla locked the Fiat and they headed in. Sean wondered if she might better remember those lines from Pascal, something about the terrifying silence of the immense night sky? But he didn't ask, and Dervla only said, 'At least we beat the milk thief this morning,' lifting the four litres at the door.

Murphy greeted them quietly, tail wagging, but Sean waved the dog back onto its bean bag in the kitchen before going upstairs. The third step from the top creaked as always, only this time Sean resolved to peel back the carpet and drive a nail, as good and true as any man, into the loose board in the morning. He could hear Dervla giving her mother a full report in the box room as he went into the twins' bedroom, only to see that they had once again slept through. He was back in bed himself by the time Dervla returned to their room, both of them once again far too wide awake to sleep. Only this time they made love, as silently as possible, yet with more abandon than Sean felt they had managed in a long time. As if they were trying to assert something against the magnitude of what they had glimpsed upon awakening, fighting fire with fire as it were, answering thanatos with eros if you like. And just as they brought one another to a shuddering climax, the first of the large feathery grey ashes from the Convent fire began to fall outside, began to fall like snow in the dark. Unbeknownst to them both, like a thief in the night, falling onto the front garden and all over the patio out back.

MARTHA'S STREETS

Dermot Bolger

Martha's hand was so stiff that writing was now impossible, but she could still read very slowly by concentrating with a magnifying glass. Once she could read she could escape from this nursing home on the outskirts of Dublin, she could turn a page and be back amid the streets of her city and James Joyce's city. She could stand on the Dublin Quays to encounter the passing faces that her own father had known. She could ignore pitiful sounds from the day room, where the other patients meekly waited for death or their dinner, and hear again the calls of gulls and hawkers over the Liffey at low tide.

The important thing about being ninety-one was not to get frustrated or to panic. Her bedroom light would be put out soon, although she had little chance of sleep. Strangers kept her awake, wandering through her room at night. The night nurse denied this and claimed that Martha was always asleep whenever she checked her. But that was because the nurses expected patients to sleep soundly, with all the patients drugged except for Martha. She was the only one with her wits left, the only one to cause trouble and make the staff laugh. Not that she was complaining because everybody was kind. Adjusting to nursing home life had proved difficult and – after being independent all her life – Martha did not intend to stay much longer. But she knew that she would never have survived another winter in her unheated flat in Baggot Street, crammed with books and cat food, if some concerned former pupils had not found her this place.

Still, while she appreciated their efforts, Martha had her own plans to escape. The nurse understood this and had even promised to help Martha pack when the winter ended. Spring was the best time to move. She would find a flat with loads of bookshelves beside a small shop and a library. The nurse had offered to help her pack for the past year now, always encouraging Martha to rest up for three more months to gain strength for the move. But next spring she would not be fobbed off in her determination to move to a flat with a windowsill where birds could gather. At least she would not be plagued by the curse of health inspectors there. Martha tried to stay calm because anger exhausted her, but she longed to rise from bed and open her window. She was asked to keep it shut after staff discovered that Martha was secretly leaving out bread for the birds and grew alarmed that the health inspector would close the nursing home if mice were attracted.

Her fellow patients spent their days dozing in the common room that Martha never entered. However, as Martha disliked communal activities, she knew little about them. This caused her guilt because she enjoyed meeting their visitors. Each afternoon, wrapped up in cardigans and a woollen hat, she lay on the sofa she had commandeered inside the porch where she could chat to everyone who arrived. Sometimes Matron fussed about the quantity of books the nurses needed to bring out for her. In reply Martha would quote Vicktor Frankl, like she had often quoted him to her pupils: 'Without a sense of purpose, a man will either be despairing or dangerous to himself and others.'

At ninety-one she had such little time left that each day needed to have a purpose. This evening – despite her cataracts – she would read six pages from the Sirens chapter of *Ulysses*. Lost in Joyce's words, she had relived the moments in Leopold Bloom's life as he sat in the Ormond Hotel and knew that his wife was preparing to be unfaithful with Blazes Boylan.

But she had also relived the moment in her own life when, at eighteen, she had first read this chapter in the banned book which her brother had managed to smuggle home from abroad. How many hands had the copy surreptitiously passed through before she found it behind a row of innocent-looking books on a shelf in his room? She had been a Loreto convent girl, hiding it in her school bag so that she could sit in St Stephen's Green after class, disguising the copy of *Ulysses* with a dust jacket from a *Lives of the Saints*. The shock and excitement she had felt that day in how Joyce captured the language between the two coarse barmaids. She had not liked the barmaids, but instantly recognised them as flesh and blood in a way that women were not in other books. Joyce allowed them to have thoughts that she had never known could be expressed in a book. Martha could still recall how a policeman had passed by her park bench in Stephen's Green, and she had been certain that he was going to turn and confiscate the book, dragging her back to the nuns to proclaim that she was a brazen unchristian hussy reading filth and pornography.

That was how her father considered *Ulysses* on the one occasion it was mentioned at the dinner table. Father would have felt let down if he knew she had read it. But, there again, he always felt let down after she began to think for herself. Let down by her desire to go to university, her refusal to find a respectable man and marry, her ambitions that went against everything he felt a woman should be. *Ulysses* had become her bible in those years, proof that people could think and believe differently, that there were secret lives running like a current beneath the façade of her city.

Still she regretted those years when she and Father had grown apart. Not that he had ever ceased to love her, but his baffled disappointment had been like a cancer which forced her to follow

Joyce abroad to where she could not feel the shadow
of his disapproval. She was teaching in Madrid in
1961 when a message came from her brother that
Father was dying in a Dublin nursing home.

She had returned home to visit the hospital and
sit in strained silence, unable to find common
ground with him. Returning to the neglected house
where Father lived alone, she had walked from room
to room before, on a sudden impulse, looking behind
the row of books in her brother's old bedroom.
There, wrapped in brown paper, was the edition of
Ulysses.

Next day she had brought it to the hospital and
began to read to him – not from cover to cover
because Father would have no time for Stephen
Dedalus's priggishness. But, over his protests, she
began to read about Leopold Bloom's visit to the
newspaper office crammed with hard-drinking
Dublin men of the world, and the chapter where
Bloom travels with other men to the funeral in
Glasnevin. At first Father had been belligerent,
demanding to know why she was poisoning his
mind. But then human curiosity kicked in. These
were his streets, his type of men. He confessed that
as young man he had once drank with Joyce's own
father, a painful case. There were expressions he
recognised. 'By god Joyce got that right,' Father
would declare suddenly. Or, 'I know the very man
he's talking about.'

In those weeks before he died *Ulysses* had given
them a common world to share – the world that
Martha had read about and her father had grown
up in. The book had helped them to know each

other in a new way. But that was the secret of *Ulysses*. It became her calling card to the world, like walking into an unknown café and placing down a chessboard. Always someone came forward. At first people in Dublin were shocked to see her reading it, after she settled here when Father died. But then young people began to approach her in Bewley's café, curious about the book that was still not sold in Irish shops back then.

The joy of the book was that it could be reread forever. As she grew older she read *Ulysses* in airports and on foreign beaches where the young were more interested in each other's bodies than in an old woman in a deckchair. Yet always someone would stop, an elderly fellow aficionado or a young girl, surprised to see it in the hands of an old woman. Occasionally the people who stopped bored her, Joyce experts frothing at a misplaced semi-colon, sucking the vitality from her father's people. Or that mad Italian in Malta who took the book as a sign that she might be interested in strange sexual games. With ordinary readers, the ones who became her friends, she could laugh about such encounters. These friends were like her in being able to move between two worlds, perpetually carrying the book in their heads. During business meetings or dutiful family occasions they could escape with Bloom into night-town or walk into eternity with Stephen along Sandymount Strand.

In recent years, when even the last of her cats had died, the people in Joyce's book became more real than the people on Dublin's streets who passed her by as she spilled change at supermarket checkouts and knew that she was boring strangers on buses. She had lived too long, with almost everyone who knew her gone. Looking in the mirror some days she barely recognised herself. The only people who never aged and who kept her sane were Joyce's characters.

But Martha knew that she was drifting into senility because the people who wandered into her room at night where not just nurses and health inspectors but characters from his book – Blazes Boylan and the Citizen and Nosy Flynn. Some nights they shouted at her and on other nights talked amongst themselves, ignoring her presence in the bed. She was going daft and knew in her heart that she would never leave here. But her plans for her death were in great order and did not include allowing her body to fall into the hands of any clergyman. It would be wonderful though if some friend played the choral finale of Beethoven's *Ode to Joy* – composed when he was so deaf that someone had to pluck his sleeve before he turned to witness the crowd's rapturous applause at the première.

Martha planned to die as she had lived, with all artifice stripped away. Yet despite her preparations, there were certain nights when death's looming closeness scared her. When would the nurse turn out her light? She needed to get asleep before the intruders starting sneaking around her room. Tomorrow somebody might call to take her out in her wheelchair. And if no one came then there was Joyce's humour to sustain her as she painstakingly reread his words with her magnifying glass.

The bedroom door opened and the nurse

appeared. The woman looked tired, but Martha hoped that with the other patients asleep there might be time to talk.

'How was your day, Martha?'

Martha looked back on the trials and frustrations and the task of reading accomplished. 'Good,' she admitted.

'So are you still leaving us?'

'When spring comes.'

'Off on your travels. You've had a few, haven't you? I was never abroad myself. We'd miss you if you went off.'

'Would you?' Martha was touched.

'Truly. You're a dote except when you get into your moods. Where did that weird poster come from?'

Martha looked up at a photograph of an impoverished looking young man seated at a bare table with a pile of roughly cut sandwiches on one side and a heap of books on the other. He was ravenously eating while devouring a book at the same time.

'I saw it years ago in Spain and had to buy it. That's what books are, food for the soul.'

'I like a good romance to curl up with myself,' the nurse said. 'Something sexy that doesn't answer back. Here, let me tuck you in till you're snug as a bug in a rug.'

Martha allowed her to adjust the tight bedclothes. 'Do me a favour, open the window.'

'Aren't you the one always complaining about the east wind? And you know you can't leave out bread for the birds.'

'I know. Just for a minute. There's something I want to hear.'

The nurse shook her head in good-humoured exasperation. Still she opened the window and stood back to listen before shaking her head.

'You see? There's nothing to hear.'

'There is.' Martha closed her eyes to listen to the night's luxuriant silence, the infinite possibilities of unheard sound from which the deaf Beethoven had stolen his marvellous notes. 'There's a whole symphony out there.'

The night nurse listened too, then closed the window. 'Maybe you're right and the rest of us are daft. I don't know. Goodnight, Martha.'

Martha didn't reply or open her eyes even when the door closed. She wanted to hold on to the still, majestic chords of the earth at peace and to hear, in faint whispers, the echoes rising from the distant Dublin streets, all those voices and thwarted lives that Joyce had captured. That intimate universe she loved, which would joyously live in other people's minds after her ashes were scattered on her father's grave, yards from where Bloom had once stood in Glasnevin cemetery.

BENNY GETS THE BLAME

Clare Boylan

Our neighbourhood was famous.
Kimmage was the first place in the
world to invent ice pops. There was a
sweet shop called Murt Scutcheons and
oul' Scutcheons had a shed out the back
where he made his own ice pops. They
tasted brutal – like lead and cough
bottle. The colours were brilliant, but.
We used to creep up behind girls and
stick them down the back of their
jumpers. If you could keep them there
long enough they went kind of mushy
and when you put them in your mouth
they crumpled like the icebergs that
sank the Titanic.

Then kids started dropping like
flies. There was mothers weeping and
wailing, thinking it was the scarlet fever
or the black plague, but it was the

lollies. It's a funny thing about mothers. You'd never even know they liked kids until they're nearly dyin' and then they love them.

Oul' Scutcheons became known as the Kimmage poisoner. His shed out the back was closed down by the health wallahs. After that we had to wait until real ice lollies were invented. The funny thing was, it didn't affect Mr Scutcheons' business. We saw him as a kind of pioneer. If any of the kids had of died, he would have been world famous.

Our mammy was another living legend. She was small but she was quare savage. She once laid out five guys. She didn't hate everything, but. Operations, she loved. You'd want to hear her and the women whisperin' on the street: '*She had it all out.*' There was oul' ones on our street with nothing left inside of them at all – like sucked eggs they were. Give you the creeps. Men never had operations. They just fell down from the drink.

Me da's temper was nearly as bad as me ma's. I used to wish that one cheek of my bum could be marked 'home' and the other 'school'. That way there might be enough flesh left on me arse to sit down. I never minded, but. Nobody really bothered me – except the sister.

Sisters is evil. When they have money they never even spend it. They make money baby-sitting. Guys can't get work baby-sitting and it's not fair cos anyone could do it. All you have to do it wipe the chiseller's tail-end and stick a soother in its gob and put your feet up on the sofa and guzzle lemonade. It used to drive us guys crazy. We'd come around and peer in the window and pull faces at them.

Then we'd feck a few apples and leg it over the wall. You'd think, now, the girls would get the blame as they were in charge of the gaff. They were real sneaky, but. When the oul' one got home – even before she handed over the shilling – the sister would say, straight out, 'Please Missus O'Toole, I have to tell you, some boys got over the wall and stole apples.' And Mrs O'Toole would say, nice as pie, 'What boys would those be, dear?' And before you could swally a gobstopper, the sister'd be in floods of tears and reel off the names and yours truly gets a roasted bum.

It's always been the same, right back to the olden times. Me and Dekko went to see this brilliant picture called *Ben-Hur*. Ben-Hur is this big guy in a little skirt and he's the chap. The villain is Stephen Boyd and he's an Irishman, only in the picture he is a Roman tribune and he used to be Ben-Hur's best mate. Well one day, there's this big parade of the Romans and Benny's out watching it from the roof with his ma and his sister. Next thing, the sister, Tirza, leans out too far and knocks a slate flying and it catches some geezer on the bonce. Now, fair play, she was the one knocked the slate. You'd say she'd be the one to get a roasted bum. Not on your nelly. It's Benny gets the blame.

Ben-Hur was the best picture ever made. Me and Dekko seen it three times. We didn't watch it all the way through. We left before the bit where Tirza and the mother is sent to live among the leopards and their noses gets eaten off and then Jesus puts them back on. It was the chariot race, but.

Now, they didn't have racing cars in the olden

times so they had races with chariots. That's a little cart-type affair with big wheels and four horses in front and the guy stands up in it and lashes the horse and they go like the clappers. Our Benny was the best of them all, but your man, Missala, he was mad jealous, so what does he do only puts these spike yokes on the wheels of his chariot, and it cuts the tripes out of the other chariots. There's horses flyin' and chaps dyin' and then it's between Benny and Missala. The messer Missala starts lashin' Benny with his whip. Only Benny's no daw — doesn't he grab the whip so that Missala's yanked out of the chariot and he gets mangled.

Well, we'd seen the picture three times. We had no more money and we couldn't think what else to do. Then I got an idea. You know when you get an idea and you feel certain it's the best idea in the whole history of the world. It makes you feel kind of peaceful. 'Dekko, my man,' I said. 'We are going to have a chariot race!'

'Feck's sake!' Dekko said, real excited. 'Where are we goin' to get chariots?'

The eejit! Where did he think we were going to get the chariots? I hadn't a clue. But I still had this kind of glow from having had the brilliant idea and I thought if I just stayed real still I would hear a voice in my head. Sure enough, the message came, sort of booming and low.

'Prams,' says I. 'We're goin' to run a chariot race with prams.'

'Janey!' Dekko says. 'With chisellers inside?'

Tell the God's truth, I hadn't thought about chisellers, but prams always has chisellers inside.

What's the point of a pram without a chiseller?

'With chisellers.'

Now, some of the guys had nippers right in their own houses but Dekko and me had none. We knew right off that no oul' one would give us a loan of her chiseller. Who else could we get them off?

The sisters! The baby-sitters!

The sisters was bigger than us. They were turning into real mots. Even though they were still stupid and scaldy, there was older guys making eyes at them. We found out which ones fancied them. Then we wrote out notes that said: 'Dear Frank (or Shamey), I will be baby-sitting at O'Tooles (or wherever) next Saturday night. Apart from baby Laurence we will have the house to ourselves. You can visit if you like. Love, Imelda.' Then we go up to these guys, all innocent, and say, 'I have a note for you from me sister.'

The night of the race the guys that has their own chisellers is lined up in the Blind Lane. Me and Dekko puts on a disguise and waits at the houses where the sisters are. Sure enough, Frank and Shamey show up, ears all washed and hair oiled. And, bingo! The sisters lets them in. We wait until they're all cosy on the sofa and then we knock on the door. 'We are the forces of righteousness!' we shout. 'We have caught you in an occasion of sin!'

'Francie, you little toe-rag!' the sister greets. (The mouth of her! How did she recognise me anyway?) 'Is that my good stocking on your head? What the feck do you want?'

'The loan of baby O'Toole,' says I.

'You want your ears ripped off,' says she.

'I'll tell me ma,' says I.

In the normal run of things sisters wouldn't be scared of anyone, but everyone is scared of our ma. 'What would you want the babby for?'

'We're having a little game,' says I. 'Me and the guys.'

'What sort of game?'

'Spot the difference. We swap the babby's hats and take bets to see who can tell which chiseller is which.'

She stands there tapping her toe. 'Well, Mrs O'Toole's only gone to the sodality. She'll be home in half an hour. You'd better have the babby back or I'll rip your head off.'

She stuffs a little knitted hat on the perisher, puts him in his pram and hands him over. Meanwhile, Dekko is legging it to the lane with the Mangan heir.

We line up at the top of the lane, real close. It's brilliant, because there is barely room for the five of us together. Dekko's younger brother, Mickser, keeps gotchie and when the coast is clear he shouts 'go' and we all go like the clappers.

The wheels is whistling and creaking. The perishers is peering out from their little pixies, kind of stunned and excited. We're goin' like the wind. I am Fangio in a Maserati. I am Benny the Hur flogging my horse to victory. To me left is the evil Roman tribune, Carrots. I can see the silver spikes on his wheels, ready to cut the tripes out of me. I give his chariot a little nudge and put on an extra spurt. I am going at a lick. The laurel wreath is mine.

Only, something happens on the blind bend.

We're goin' too fast to keep the chariots straight. Carrots Twomey is losing the bend. His legs is all over the place. Honest to God, its like that feckin' pram has a life of its own. It plunges into all the other chariots. There's this brutal pile-up, prams mangled. All the little perishers inside begins to wail – not real loud or anything, but like, a bit despairing. Meanwhile, I am the only one to attempt avoidance action, sadly ineffective. Me wheels head straight for the wall. The pram is banjaxed. The perisher shoots out. He hits the earth without a sound. He looks kind of surprised, if you can look surprised with your eyes closed. 'Is he dead?' Mickser says. And I don't know. I never seen anyone dead.

He opens his little eyes. He opens his little mouth. He begins to bawl. The lungs of him! Never in the entire history of the world have roars been heard the like of it – until, that is, there is another, even worse, bleedin' blood-curdling yell.

'My baby! What have you done to my baby?' It's Mrs O'Toole. She's headin' our way. We can't do nothin'. We just look at each other, kind of haunted. How did she know it was her babby?

We often used to think about baby O'Toole. The chariot race, which remained the greatest achievement of my career, ended with a sore head for him and a sore bum for me (the sister's skinny rear – need you ask – stayed as white as a wood pigeon's egg). I couldn't sit down for a month. It was worse for him. I don't keep my brains in my arse. He turned out quare all right. When he was still crawlin' he used to walk around with his eyes glued to the ground, looking for halfpennies. By the time he was seven he'd sell you a Woodbine, take a drag on it himself, tell you how much money he'd saved and say that when he grew up, he'd have enough to buy Kimmage. Poor little Toolser. We knew the brain was banjaxed. Who the feck would want to buy Kimmage?

THE SUNDAY FATHER

Frank McGuinness

My father died on the same Sunday as Princess Diana. His distraught wife rang to tell me the news. I was not distraught but I did offer her my condolence. She gave me details about the body and its burial. I listened carefully, noting it all down, for I hadn't the heart or the desire to tell this stranger I wouldn't be going.

The tickets were booked and our clothes packed before I had changed out of my pyjamas and showered. I fed our twins, Beth and Simon, their favourite mashed banana. I'd beaten the fruit to a delicious pulp. They are smiling babies except when they eat; then they look solemn as scarecrows. I've seen babies devour food as if it will be grabbed from them. Both of mine eat with no sense of hurry, sure that they will be allowed to clean their plates. That is why it took me so long to get dressed. That morning my priority was to see my children did not go hungry.

Honoria organised our usual minder. Absolutely understood she couldn't expect notice, ghastly shock, everything would be fine for a few days, a week if we liked, this wonderful woman assured us. And she was sorry to hear about my father. Yes, terrible news, shattering, quite shattering, you're so good to take both, Ria gushes on the phone. But she adores them, no trouble. When Ria comes back into the kitchen, I notice two little golden beads of sweat on her forehead. Her red hair is unruly. All done, she sighs, and leans back against the sink. Get a move on, get ready, she advises.

I don't want to get ready. It is Sunday. I want to make love. I want to throw my red golden beautiful wife to the cold ground of our tiled kitchen, I want to smear mashed banana over her hard flesh, I want to fuck our brains out all day till we have satisfied every terrifying desire and one of us is crying, sobbing our hearts out with pain. I want what I cannot have. Right, I'll get a move on. Do, do, we don't have that much time. I have a sudden idea. Maybe we should take them with us. Take the twins to Dublin.

—Why?

—He's not seen them. He probably would want to.

—You mean your father? He's dead. How can he see them?

—Must have forgotten.

—Just get dressed.
—All right.

The mourning for the dead princess I expected in London, but the Irish surprised me. It was all I heard them talking about in the airport. If they were not camouflaging their sorrow behind the newspapers, they were openly lamenting in conversation with each other. What's happened to the Irish, why have they stopped hating? Ria inquired. I could not help. I was busy wondering how strangers could be so genuinely tearful — and it was real tears I saw them shed — at the death of a woman who in life would not piss on them if their trousers were on fire. The man who bred me and left me, my father, had died that morning. I could not stir up from inside me an ounce of sorrow. How would the little princes, William and Harry, how would they manage without a mother? They have a father, I interrupted one conversation, and it must have been too sharp, for the women stopped talking and looked at me as if I had barked and bit them.

I was tempted to throw my head back and howl just to see the effect such a manifestation of faked grief would have on the two, but I resisted. What is the point of entertaining with extravagant gestures when you're never going to set eyes on the bastards again and cannot appreciate their fearfulness recollected in tranquillity? This pack of dungbags boarding our plane was driving me to demented distraction, churning my stomach into stinking sticky salted butter spread thickly on stale bread. Full of nothing but its own fat. My legs too were turning into that rancid mess, melting as we walked into the heart of the aircraft.

I would have loved to use my boot to clear off the shits lamenting Diana's death. Even to tread on their toes. To give them genuine pain. A real reason to weep. To stop their smell so that I would not have to get on the plane and be surrounded by them in that place of their excrement. Today I cannot, I must fly. Ria looked at me early that morning. You are going to Dublin. Don't try any excuses. We will be at your father's funeral. I can book tickets and pack in five minutes. That is that.

I calm myself on the flight. I imagine Beth and Simon lie in my arms. The two of them may weigh a ton together but I don't mind. Bethy always cries when we try to get her to sleep. Beth-Bethy-Bathsheba, I'd whisper. Bathsheba is what I wish we'd called her, though Simon was Simon from the start. Ria said she might suffer at school from so oddly biblical a name. I argued that it was not as if we were going to send her to school at Nazareth, so we settled on the more acceptably Jewish Elizabeth. I now adore Elizabeth because it belongs to my beautiful daughter, and for her in the future I wish all the diversities and differences her name can transform itself into – Beth, Bessie, Eliza, Eilish, Ella, Lizzie, Lisa, Liza, Eileen and a million more if she so wishes. I wonder which of these my dead father would have settled on for his granddaughter. Probably he would have called her that crying child. That eternally crying child. Put a sock in it. Take the strap to her. Slam a shoe over her arse and that will shut her crying. The slap of a slipper across her face will quieten the bitch.

Do not touch my baby. She is trying to sleep in my arms. Together with her twin brother. I will sing to them. I start to hum. Ria is curious. What are you singing? Nothing. I am embarrassed at the sound of my voice, so I sing silently to my son and daughter who are now beginning to enjoy their invisible sleep.

> On wings of the wind over the rolling deep
> Angels are coming to watch over thy sleep,
> Angels are coming to watch over thee
> So listen to the wind coming over the sea.
> Hear the wind blow, love, hear the wind blow.
> Lean your head over and hear the wind blow.

My daughter wakes up crying. The little boy wakes up too. I try to comfort them by rocking to and fro, saying, please, little ones, please don't cry, what's making you cry?

They answer in voices strangely, savagely adult for two-year-old children. Beth blames me for singing such a sad song. That was what made her cry. It also turns out that I had offended Simon's sense of metrics. He points out that in the Connemara Cradle Song, my lullaby, I have misused the word 'over' three times. It is 'o'er the rolling deep', 'o'er thy sleep', 'o'er the sea'. This is precisely what the anonymous lyricist composed. He uses the two syllable 'over' in the last line. Had he intended two syllables earlier, he would have done so. Also the archaic 'list' is preferable to 'listen', and 'list to the wind' is more beautiful than the barbarous carnage I have inflicted on their infant ears.

I listen to this tedious nitpicking with good grace. They are still babies really. Such pedantry at that age is quite an endearing trait. Peering at me through horn-rimmed bottle-glassed spectacles, their breath reeking of morning sherry, they burst into tears, having assembled about them a group of likeminded academic young ladies, sweet in blue stockings, one of whom is devoted to gathering what monies you can spare for a charity dedicated to the relief of suffering distressed gentlefolk now suffering in greater and greater numbers. Her name, she reveals, is Princess Diana, whose gentle face deserved a softer death than being squashed like a melodeon in a Paris tunnel. I can hear the crash, the car ballooning, the baying of mad dogs. Noise makes the glass of water in my hand fly from me. Luckily the spill drenches only my own person. Ria and the kind air hostess towel me down. He's fine. I'm fine. No harm done. What were you thinking of? Leave me alone, for God's sake, I want to say. Instead I thank Ria for organising all of this. She does not smile as I want her to smile. Instead, she is quite serious. She says, that's fine but maybe you were right. Maybe we should have brought Simon and Bathsheba.

Jesus, this city, how do I hate thee, let me count the ways. I hate the stench of Dublin filling my nostrils as I take the first step on this hard soil. I contain myself, I stop the smell, my brain is bigger than my body. I decide that I hate the exchange of money in this filthy temple of this filthy city in this filthy country. I suggest we pay for everything in sterling, pound on par for punt, and my wife puts me up against a wall. She declares enough is enough. These are our hard-earned wages. She will not allow herself to be ripped off, not by me, not by any chancer – get that out of my lazy, lousy brain. I have put up with your shit too much already this day, she hisses. Absolutely no more. Do I understand that? Because if I don't she will get on the next available flight to London. Go back to our children. She will leave me to die in Dublin and swear to Jesus will not come back for my funeral. Does she make herself clear?

If you do not want to do that, wait for me in the bar. Douse yourself with drink. Pour the pints into you. Welcome the fountain of good old Guinness into your hungry exile's stomach. Crash into a bottle of duty-free Black Bush. Let it rip down your throat. Catch cancer hoarding the smoke of ten thousand Sweet Afton Cigarettes safely ensconced in your dirty lungs. Die roaring for morphine and cursing the first Players No. 6 you stuck into your mouth, acting the hard man to impress the harder men studying commerce. They could win over women because for some reason they had no fear of them. And you have always been frightened of women, I imagine my wife saying. That man you kept following, my boy, the man you were obsessed with, the man you wanted to fuck, what words did he use to shake you out of his spell? He spoke them in Irish. In Gaeilge. In Erse. *An bhuil cineal eagla ort?* Is there some kind of fear in you? Fear of women. His fear, neatly diverted onto me.

I let Ria queue at the bureau de change. We get a

good deal on the exchange, thank Christ. It will be expensive standing drinks at the wake and funeral. I do not know how many friends my father had made but to be safe I am expecting many unfamiliar faces. I watch my wife walk away from the counter. If Princess Diana had ever come to Dublin, rather than gallivant through Paris, now lying cold in a morgue, she too might have stood in line to get her Irish money. They could do nothing for her in the best French hospitals and they could do nothing for my father in whatever hospital Dublin deigned to offer one of its least significant citizens. Blood stopped her breathing, and my father's heart could be cut out of his aging body and placed in her throat so she could feel her life breathing in her hands again, in her veins, her breasts, her child, her children. I think of her sons. The princes. Their savage grief to have lost their mother. I think of myself. My father's son. My utter indifference. I wished him dead and I got my wish. My father that I hate in this city I hate.

Ria joins me with our money. We catch a taxi to our city, our capital, the centre of our capital. I hate the roadworks disfiguring the endless detours. I hate the driver cracking jokes about politics. I don't fucking remember who the Taoiseach is. I do not care. So I say nothing. Ria says your man sounds like a right one. Well, he's rightly screwed us, the driver says, he's screwed Ireland. I imagine the bastard mounting the statue of Cuchulain outside the GPO. His prick blasts through the stone arse of the ancient hero and in juicy jubilation that cock can grow so monumental it bursts through Cuchulain's clay mouth, spouting poisonous sperm all through this hateful city, his disease of greed infecting the innocent, turning them into the guilty, the gutless, the bastard cowards that let Dublin become this hateful shrine to the shite that it smells of.

But my nose is sick of shit. I want no more of it. I want to go home. Where is my home? With Simon my son, my loyal son. With Bathsheba my daughter, my beautiful daughter. We're here, Ria says, we're at the hotel, you have the Irish money, pay the man! The bill is eight million roubles. Fuck it, are we in Moscow, in Petersburg, in Odessa? Why are you speaking, my good man, in that oddly Slavonic fashion? Ria pulls the wallet from my hands. My husband's father has died, he is behaving strangely. I am sorry for your troubles, the taxi man says. No, you're not, you're more sorry for the Princess of Wales, at least you know who she was. I couldn't give a fuck for her, he assures me, the English can all go to hell. I'm glad the royal family got what was coming to them. She deserved to die young – how many of ours did they take too soon? She got what they were looking for. I vomit profusely in his car, after I laughed myself sick just to let him think I agree.

He starts to scream. Bastard, bastard, get out.

He throws open the door beside me. But I decline this invitation to step outside. Instead I lean over the driver's seat and explode my guts onto where my bigoted chauffeur sat. It dances everywhere, the yellow, the green, the white, inside me, now outside. I vomit for Ireland.

He has stopped screaming. He is now crying. Big salt tears from his eyes. This fucking grown man is bawling over a car. I ask him, what is wrong? Have you lost your father? Have you lost your young wife? Have you lost your virginity? Why are you weeping and screaming as if I have defiled your life? My father left my mother and so I was defiled as an abandoned child. I recovered from this loss sufficiently well to be capable of stepping out of a cab and walking into the hotel with the express intention of checking in but my wife got there before me and did the dirty of telling them I was in need of sound sleep, that I'd be fine. Absolutely fine. I talk to the weeping driver, I say I am sorry. You have made my father's funeral much easier to bear. I wish to give you a present. I therefore take a pair of pink socks from my hand luggage and give them to him. I tell him, in Egypt this is the done thing to thank a boy for being fucked. Or indeed for fucking. He stops crying. I smile. I say, please, for you, the least I can do for destroying your beautiful car. These socks belonged to my Egyptian father. He has just died. From an excess of pink.

Am I thanked for this act of enlightened generosity? Am I buffalo. He hurls the pink socks from the window of his car, and I catch them with a skill that surprises me. The ancient Gaelic game of hurling was never my strong point. Now, a grown man, back with his wife, having fathered two children, albeit twins, I seem to have acquired a skill, a stratagem, a structure to my physical behaviour that allows me to be so quick. So accomplished, so extraordinarily capable of playing with the professionalism abhorred by those who know the game, who rule it, who appreciate the finer points of its playing.

Clearly my dying father has unleashed in me not so much a masculine grace but the leonine female strength of a good man with a sliotar in one hand and a stick in the other, arriving at that moment of triumph in a match when he becomes she and is unbeatable. I was my father's son, but when the old boy, the old fella, the old man died, I could, had I so wished, become queen of England, Scotland, Wales, Northern Ireland — the entire territory of the United Kingdom — should I have stayed with the treacherous, disloyal adulterer who was my husband.

Instead I married early. A virgin. I married a woman who sleeps, exhausted, in the afternoon, having gotten up early, arranged flights, dumped two kids, done every fucking job demanded of her: she sleeps beside me. What are her dreams?

She is with her husband. A drug dealer. He showers three, four times a day since he's given up heroin. He concentrates instead on selling, while all the time seeking by showering to be rid of the stench that is himself. No, that will not do. Next dream.

She mutilates herself as punishment for not having children. Her unhappy husband encourages this by sipping the blood from her wound, so purple, so lovely in the flow of juice. He dresses himself in her mutilation so he can be a man and a woman. He wraps himself in such fashion as he wishes for the cloths of heaven to swaddle round his wife's cunt and then he may not fuck her. He is thinking of his dying father. The same day as Princess Diana died. When he tries to breathe he finds her blonde hair inside his mouth. He finds a broken, beautiful body in the bathroom as he takes a piss. She is white, gentle soap in the hands he washes, pink English Rose in the paste against his yellowing teeth and the smell of women in her corpse as he turns to kiss his sleeping wife, at siesta, at peace, in Dublin the city he hates.

How do I hate thee, let me count the ways. I walk down Grafton Street. My – how it has changed. It is wonderful the way Dublin has turned its magical streets into my father crying like a child not to be left alone. Diana nowhere to be seen. Absolutely nowhere. I think my wife is pregnant. This would explain my behaviour.

We take the Dart to Booterstown to meet the woman who married my recently deceased father. In our pockets we carry wallets with a wad of Irish money, a little of my medication, pictures of our twins, pictures of ourselves, pictures of my father, pictures of Ria's parents, pictures of our house in London, pictures of myself at the age my father left us, pictures that go to make up life if you live by pictures. We reach the coast and get out of the Dart. I've done this before. Three times I've stood at the rusting stairway looking into the grey sea and dirty sand, wondering if he might be taking a constitutional walk along the shore and by chance bump into me. The waves would sometimes threaten to mount the stone wall and soak me, but they never did. The sea at Booterstown is well mannered. I would stand there looking out at the hard water thinking of my mother abandoned by my father, and in the seabirds' harsh voices I could hear her weeping at her cruelty in driving him away even though it was the right thing to do, for the brute beast could not keep his claws off women, any women, all women. I was once tempted to start beating my head against the wall for no good reason other than to drive their memory out of my brain, but that would not have worked. I remember everything. I stand today before crossing over, looking at the deserted strand — it is always deserted — when to my shock, two horses, one white, one brown, driven by young girls, race like lightning striking the land, scattered silver beneath their hoofs, then disappearing forever out of sight on their way towards the city submerged beneath black traffic.

—You could have knocked me down with a feather when I heard your name was the same as my own. Talk about like father like son. Two of them picking women called Ria. Of course I would say your full name is Maria. Am I right?

—It's Honoria, actually, my wife informs.

—How lovely. You'll never guess what mine is, so I'm not going to give you the trouble of guessing. I'll tell you straight. It's Rialto. I'm called after a cinema my mother had her first court in. Could you beat that? My poor sister, Lord have mercy on her, she passed herself off as Agnes but she was christened Angina. I know it's a disease, but my mother swore she was some kind of Neapolitan saint devoted to the care of the Sacred Heart. She was a cruel woman at a baptism font. But didn't we survive? And God love her, she left myself and himself lying in that coffin this lovely little house in Booterstown.

That is where we are sitting, myself, two Rias, a scrawny priest called Father Gerard and the corpse of my dead father in whose name we are gathered under this roof, hearing the click of the two clocks, watching a blank TV screen, smelling the roses on the wallpaper, the daisies on the carpet and the marigolds on the cushions. The net curtains are clean, the whole house stinks of scrubbing soap and the priest is lisping his way through another decade of the rosary. Some men might believe they have a vocation to the priesthood because of a vision, a vow, a desire to make money, a desire for security, but Father Gerard took to the collar because he was a sissy, and this vocation was as good a means of protecting his goolies from objecting boots as any other devised by God or man. He looks like a sissy, talks like one, sits like one, breathes like one. No one, as I've said, could lay a finger on him or kick the shit out of him because the bastard is both a priest and an old man. Changed times though in Dublin. Neither age nor dignity might spare him in this country where they've begun to hate the old and have always hated the clergy but were too tongue-tied, too servile, too superstitious to admit it.

The short silence between us is broken by the widow.

—So you have a little boy and a little girl. I would have loved a child, a girl, but himself would not hear of it. Begging your pardon, young man, your father had enough with the one. Nothing to do with you. All to do with your mother. I'm not speaking out of turn. You know no love was lost between them. But she broke his heart, and I could not heal it.

Father Gerard's voice minces its way through some observation on how many hearts have been broken by love, but if we turn fully to God he mends them, mends them all, alanna darling. He ends every sentence with that term of endearment. My darling alanna. My oily banana. Well I'm neither your darling nor your alanna, you banana-sucking bastard. Mercifully he announces he has to be on his way, duty calls to some toilet in Blackrock Park. He shakes my hand, his fingers like sponge in sherry trifle. This is what he would taste like as he kisses both women on the cheeks. Sweet mother of the divine and gentle fuck, he bends over the coffin and if this big bowl of yellow jelly dribbles on my dead father's face, I will stab him and strangle him with his own pink entrails or tear the tongue from his mouth descending onto the dead flesh of my father's lined, white, hairless face. His lips reach the forehead, they touch it, they seem to linger but instead they are whispering, God take you, God bless you, God love you. And God forgive you, I add but no one takes me up.

The priest leaves. The three of us relax a little. It is clear my father's widow is glad to see the back of the clergy. She is smiling. She eyeballs me.

—Did you know your father had a great sense of fun? Especially with women. He wasn't dirty but he could make the ladies scream. I remember once in a pub in Blackrock. It was called the Dolphin then, what it's called now God knows. Every Saturday night we had a singsong. One evening's end your father, he hurled back his head and he roared —

Let your wind blow, girls, let your wind blow,
Throw your leg over and let your wind blow.

Then he would pretend to fart. The gang of us would die laughing. The night would finish with me and him singing. Do you know our song?

From the candy store on the corner
To the chapel on the hill
Two young lovers are dying to go there
And they dream some day they will.

All hands would be very quiet, considering our circumstances. Depending on how much we'd downed, there might not be a dry eye in the pub, but nobody ever said anything.

The face in the coffin does not smile or cry or sing. He is my father of whom I know fuck all, care less. To this old woman he is the flower of her forest now plucked and withered. He smells of orchids rare as the love between them that lasted through their life together and our life apart.

—Do you hate me? she questions.

—Yes, I did, I answer.

—Do you still?

—I don't think so, no.

—Good.

Again she eyeballs me, her blue watery pupils still capable of piercing.

—Life's too short. Jesus, look at Princess Diana, poor girl. Such a lovely young woman, her life smashed to pieces. But enough about her, we have our own grieving, haven't we? You must be wondering something. Why are we not inundated with friends and family? I know in Donegal the wakes are black with people, folk coming out your ears. You must think Dubliners very bad neighbours. Not so, my man. Your mother's funeral was like Grafton Street on Christmas Eve I'm told – mind you, she was buried on a Sunday, plenty there just going to mass. I've insisted on house private. It's looking very stuck up but when it's always been just the two of you, it's nice to spend the last hours together with no one to bother you. It's a surprise to me the two of yous came over from London, such bother and expense, but I had to tell you, for of course you had the right to see him. Should I make tea? Would you like some tea? I don't think he hated you. Rest assured –

—He broke my mother's heart.

—I'm sorry to interrupt you, she interrupts. That is just nonsense. I want to show you something. Look what I've hidden under the stairs.

She opens a press door.

—What do you think of that?

We look in and see it. A crossbow.

—Jesus Christ, Ria says, what is –

—A crossbow. He saved up and bought it on the quiet. He'd always wanted one and a few years ago he figured out why. He imagined it must be the cruellest death, to go by crossbow. That was how he was going to top your mother off. How much he hated her. Lucky enough I stumbled on it searching for our plastic Christmas tree. That's where we stored it and I almost fainted when I came upon that contraption. I spelt it out to him. The only way he would not spend his last days in Mountjoy would be to plead insanity, and only a sane man could have managed to fire this boyo. Isn't it terrifying? Would it not put the heart crosswise in you? I'm sure he wanted you to have it. The man was never practical when it came to presents. How would you get that past airport security in the times that are in it? You see, no sense when it came to giving – I was nearly landed one birthday with an anaconda just because I was foolish enough to admire one on David Attenborough's programme. Again pure luck – I found out in time and put the foot down. Me or the anaconda. Choose. Innocent he was, in that way. I know what I'll do. You have a son. I'll save it for him here, the crossbow. When he's man big he might be allowed then to travel on planes with such things. You have a bit of a cross face on you. Have I offended you?

—How could he have hated my mother so much?

—To want to murder her? Tit for tat in a way. She wanted rid of him. She had you as consolation for his loss. In fact if you want the truth, your father told me, after you were born, she had her son and he'd done his job as far as she was concerned. He could bugger off. She banished him from the bed, that's for sure. He upped and went to Dublin. He got a job in the docks and was in digs near Monkstown. I met him through my brother. Jesus, your da was a broken piece of work then. She'd demolished him well. That bitch – don't deny it, bitch she was – she had ridiculed him into believing everything he did was wrong. Everything he touched would smash. She left him barely a man at all. I'll never forget the first time I touched him between the legs. He got such a shock I thought he'd crack in two. His nerves were shot, but I had a kind word for him and a gentle hand. It was all he needed. He was soon in my bed. We lived as husband and wife and nobody knew any different. I made a man out of the drink of water your whitred of a mother discarded.

My father continues to lie peacefully in his coffin, not contradicting her, not standing up for himself or his own, not smiling, giving nothing away as she lights four candles at each compass point of the coffin and throws a torrent of holy water onto the corpse.

—That will waken him if he's only letting on he's dead for a laugh, she says, starting to sing the Connemara Cradle Song over his corpse.

Ria my wife has been saying nothing. She just eyes me like a hawk. I would like to think my silence worries her. But that's not the look on her face. Instead I'd swear she is enraged. Her mouth has the tight squeeze I loathe. It is the look of her mother watching her brothers down more than two beers. It is the look of a woman who wants alcohol but may deny it fiercely. Were I to see that expression permanently on her face it would eventually turn my heart to stone and kill me.

—If you don't want tea, how about a whiskey or a bottle of stout? It's all I've got in the house. All your father would drink. Would you like a sherry, Ria?

—I'll have a whiskey, Ria answers, and if it's all right I'll pour it myself. She starts to open presses searching for drink and finds it pretty easily.

—Help yourself, good woman, the widow suggests.

—I will, my wife replies, if I may be so bold. I

hope you don't mind me being forward, seeing how you've called my husband's mother all the names of the day. But I can understand how a lady like herself must have been so bitter. That woman was a warrior. She tried to drive a JCB through our marriage bed. Her main method of disruption was the scare of her catching cancer. When she did die, it did come as a shock that she eventually succumbed to a strange ringing in her ears, an incessant pounding of extraordinary noises largely emitting from her heart that the poor women insisted was moving with absolute licence through her body. She could hear it beating in her ears, her throat, even on one occasion, that I witnessed myself, in her feet, causing her to dance like a being possessed in the bloodstream by the rhythm of her heart.

—She jived till she died, the widow rhymed.

—I cannot say for sure, Ria politely ignored the joke, but it may have been that exertion which caused my poor husband's mother to pass away. I believe she went cursing me for stealing her sad son from her arms, dividing mother from child as she divided father from child, but I cannot confirm or deny this ironical twist as the unfortunate matron expired minutes, yes a matter of seconds, before we arrived in her rather impressive abode in Donegal. A self-made woman who made her pile running single-handedly the first supermarket to open in her home town – people used to come just to see the checkout machine. Innocent times indeed. She was well respected there, you know, not least because she dumped the useless fucker you devoted the past years of your life to serving.

Weren't you the fool? Do you know, I'll have another whiskey.

Then Ria did something remarkable as she poured her drink. I was stunned to hear her sing. The first time I discovered my wife had the loveliest, sweetest, barely audible soprano voice. There she was, cradling her glass, finishing the refrains of that Connemara lullaby.

The currachs are sailing way out of the blue
Chasing the herring of silvery hue.
Silver the herring and silver the sea
Soon they'll be silver for my love and me.

Ria joined voices with Ria. Their soft gave way to their harsh unison.

Let your wind blow, girls, let your wind blow,
Throw your leg over and let your wind blow.

Then they farted with their mouths and their faces were like bulldogs smelling each other's arses. I was visibly shaken. In my quiet way I like women to be women and from what little I knew of Father, I genuinely believe he would have agreed with me. In the day that was in it I also feel duty bound to point out that such vulgarity was not Princess Diana's way. An adulteress, yes, a foolish virgin before she married, yes, whose manners and breeding led to the bloody farce of her death, yes, but God was sufficiently enamoured of her not to leave her decapitated as he did Jayne Mansfield in her car crash all those years ago. He must have approved of Diana, for I can remember a devout Christian of my acquaintance laughing hysterically at that headless image of poor

Miss Mansfield, laughing with such relish that it was clear only after the moment of her death could this sad bag of shit wank about her. Avoid such Christians and avoid all talk of Diana or decapitation of the female form when two such women are hitting the bottle the way Ria and Ria were doing. I pretend to close my eyes and sleep as they prattle.

—Has himself fallen asleep? the widow inquires.

—He might have, my wife equivocates.

—His father had the same habit, her opponent taps fingers against a glass.

—It's a bad one, my wife decrees.

—There's worse, Rialto contradicts.

—What?

—His father used to hide the drink, Rialto confesses.

—Your late husband? (Who the fuck else, I feel like interjecting.)

—Himself, she enlightens.

—You let him?

—I had to. He was a terrible man if you crossed him. (My mother could confirm that.)

—You were a martyr, Honoria, canonises my father's wife.

—A martyr to his moods, she elaborates.

—What would you do to get drunk?

—Go down to the off-licence and buy it, she admits.

—That's what I do too, she whispers as if they were thieving.

—Uncanny, the widow returns the whisper.

—We were meant to meet, Ria, my wife ponders the role of fate.

—Thank God I made that phonecall, the widow prefers to believe in a benevolent divinity.

—He wasn't going to come, the treacherous bitch lets it out of the bag.

—Why not? (It is a challenge.)

—His dead mother, the hateful woman tells all.

—Fuck her, says the widow who did not go to finishing school.

—Our son and little daughter, sad his father never saw them, my evil wife begins to sob.

—Bless them. Does he love her? (What about him?)

—He loves me, Honoria is now letting tears fall.

—His father loved me, the widow joins in the weeping aria.

—And he's dead, the cruel wagon reminds her.

—She took him from me, Rialto blames my unfortunate mother.

—Who did?

—His fucking whore of a first wife. When she died.

—From the grave? My strange wife learns of things that trouble her.

—Where she belonged. She waited. She wanted him, the widow indulges herself.

—How do you know that, Ria?

—She told him. He told me. His dying breath. She pours more whiskey.

—What did he say? My wife downs her drink.

—She's looking, she's laughing, she's giving me her disease, the widow follows suit.

—The sounds she was hearing? My wife pours more whiskey.

—In her heart – the very same. Calling him from mine into her arms.

—She was jealous, my wife states the obvious, what did she say?

—It wasn't just what she said. It was the way she looked, Rialto grows mysterious.

—How did she look?

—She took the shape of Princess Diana, the widow's face is grey as her hair.

—That's not possible. My wife is glad she wore black as the rooms dims.

—She kept telling my dying husband her marriage killed her.

—She asked him for help?

—She told him she had two children. He loved children. Again the widow sobs.

—Not his own. He didn't love his own son. My wife is on my side.

—True, but he took pity on this beautiful girl and died to keep her company.

—As she travelled across the river Styx.

—In a boat? Rialto inquires, ignoring the allusion.

—It must have been.

—At least it wasn't the number 7 bus.

—What is that?

—It goes to Sallynoggin.

—I don't know it. (I am certain my wife is exhausted.)

—Tell me this and tell me no more, the widow is testing my wife.

—Another whiskey?

—Pour – pour – pour, she urges generously.

—What's your question?

—When I take the number 7 bus it's full of Chinese —

—What about them? (Honoria begins to fear Rialto is racist.)

—So many Chinese people on that one bus, the widow observes.

—What's your problem?

—The bus can take eighty-one people —

—What is the matter with you?

—How can billions of Chinese fit in to the one double decker?

—Is that what it seems like to you? Do you see them in their billions?

—I do.

—Then God love your eyes, Honoria blesses the other woman.

By this stage of their conversation I am still pretending to sleep as they sip whiskey, not noticing a strange noise disturbing the calm of the corphouse. It looks as if only I can witness it. My father has left his coffin. He has heard enough of the women's endless tattle. He has decided such stuff is not for him. As he did in life, finite life, he leaves, choosing not this discourse of fair ladies as his infinity, his destiny. Yes, he fucks off, leaving those behind to manage as well they might. The girls, so absorbed in their mourning, their drinking, in their perfectly reasonable denial of logic, need not notice the dead man slipping away, no more than my mother did when he scrammed from their bed, despite my calling, daddy, daddy, where are you going? Why are you leaving us? What did I do?

If he hears us, he does not answer. If he does not hear, then he is not there. If he is not there, then he may not ever have been, and neither might I nor any of us. The girls by this time are lighting more candles. They have started to pour Irish whiskey over the empty coffin. Ria and Ria kiss each other. They swear eternal friendship. They dance. I watch them. Then they study photographs of our children. My son is called after my father, I hear Ria tell his widow. Then they resume dancing and the tiny lad comes leaping into their dance. The ghost of my father reappears, seen by only me and my boy. Daddy lifts a candle and lets hot wax fall onto my poor little boy's fat legs. They are scarred by the fire my father leaves behind him, my soft son, crying like a girl, like a boy, and I walk away, because to do otherwise would be to pet and confuse him.

I hear him scream for his daddy. Father. It is the Sabbath, I explain. I cannot hold you. But I do explain to him that I have died and I have an appointment with a member of the British royal family. She too has died this morning and by reason of courtesy, she must have priority over all common attachments. That is how things work in the country of shades. I hear my little boy say he will sing me a song if I come back. I let him sing.

The minstrel boy to the war has gone,
In the ranks of death you'll find him.
His father's sword he has girded on
And his wild harp slung behind him.
Land of song said the warrior bard
Though all the world betray thee

One sword at least thy light shall guard,
One faithful harp shall praise thee.

As I listen to this childhood voice, I realise I will
remember his gentle face forever, but I turn my back
and beg him to forgive me, since he can never forget
me. On the other hand we all have our problems.
Fuck him. Sing on, sonny boy, you'll be a tougher
man for it.

The minstrel fell, but the foeman's chain
Could not bring his proud soul under,
The harp he loved n'er spoke again
For he tore its chords asunder
And said, no chains shall sully thee,
Thou soul of love and bravery.
Thy songs were made for the pure,
They shall never sound in slavery.

Lulled by this lament, the women now sit in a
stupor. Hand in hand. They sit listening to sudden
rain, glass clattering against glass. They say they're
glad to be inside this night. They still do not notice
my dead father has gone missing outside in the
torrent flooding the dry streets, the lanes, the tree-
lined avenue of Booterstown, valley of willows and
mistletoe, unkissed men and women, bending the
yew and sycamore, tragic creatures of the forest
giving refuge to the moving limbs of my father's
corpse, miraculously flexible now, stirred into his
second life as animal, vegetable, mineral, drinking
the earth's sustenance through the damp black and
blue of the clay they might have shovelled on the
pale wood of his coffin, had he not decided to do

a runner. Should I tell them a miracle has occurred? A man has risen from the dead? I decide to delay the Messiah moment. They'd only fly into a panic. They'd want to search for the body. Where on earth could they begin? Where could they find him? It is the dark of night. Let us wait till Sabbath, the Sunday father passes. Then we'll see.

Ivy Bannister's stories have won the Francis MacManus and Hennessy Awards, and have been collected in *Magician* (1996). Her radio play *The Wall* received the Mobil Ireland Playwrighting Award, and her poetry appears regularly in Irish periodicals. Born in New York, she has lived in Ireland since 1970, and received a doctorate from Trinity College, Dublin.

Maeve Binchy is internationally known for her best-selling novels, which include *Light a Penny Candle*, *Circle of Friends*, and her most recent work, *Nights of Rain and Stars*. In addition to her novels, she has published several collections of short stories, as well as plays. She is at work on a new novel, and lives in County Dublin.

Dermot Bolger is an award-winning poet, playwright and novelist whose works include *Father's Music* and *The Lament for Arthur Cleary*, which received the Samuel Beckett Prize. The founder of Raven Arts Press, he also co-founded New Island in 1992. He has been Playwright in Association with The Abbey Theatre and Writer Fellow in Trinity College, Dublin.

Born in Dublin, **Clare Boylan** has received awards for her journalism and her fiction, which includes *Holy Pictures*, *Home Rule* and two collections of short stories. Her latest novel, *Emma Brown*, is a continuation of an eighteen-page fragment written by Charlotte Brönte before her death. She lives in County Wicklow.

Roddy Doyle is the author of seven acclaimed novels, including *The Commitments*, *A Star Called Henry* and *Paddy Clarke Ha Ha Ha*, which won the Booker Prize in 1993. He has also written several childrens' books, several plays, and a memoir of his parents, *Rory And Ita*. *Oh, Play That Thing*, his most recent novel, was published in 2004.

Born in Boston, **Anthony Glavin** came to Ireland in 1974, where he has worked as the editor of New Irish Writing, at the *Irish Press*, and as a commissioning editor for New Island. He is the author of the story collections *One for Sorrow* and *The*

Draughtsman and the Unicorn, and *Nighthawk Alley,* his highly-praised first novel.

Desmond Hogan has published five novels, including *A Curious Street* and *A Farewell To Prague,* and two books of stories, *The Mourning Thief* and *Lebanon Lodge.* The recipient of the John Llewellyn Rhys Memorial Prize and a DAAD fellowship in Berlin, he will publish a collection of stories in 2005.

A member of Aosdana, **Bernard MacLaverty** has published four collections of stories and four novels, the latest of which is *The Anatomy School,* and has adapted his fiction for other media. Among his honours and awards are The Saltire Book of the Year and the short-list for the Booker Prize (for *Grace*).

Colum McCann has published two story collections and three novels, most recently the highly acclaimed *Dancer.* He has received the Pushcart and Rooney Prizes and the Hennessy Award, and has been an IMPAC finalist. In 2002 he was named the first winner of the Princess Grace Memorial Literary Award. He lives in New York with his wife and children.

Frank McGuinness's Tony and Olivier award-winning plays include *Observe the Sons of Ulster Marching Towards the Somme, Someone Who'll Watch Over Me, Dolly West's Kitchen* and *Speaking Like Magpies.* He is the author of three poetry collections, and has adapted plays by Lorca, Ibsen, Chekov and Brecht. Lecturer in English at University College Dublin, he lives in County Dublin.

Joseph O'Connor's novels include *Cowboys and Indians, Desperadoes, The Salesman, Inishowen* and *Star of the Sea,* a 2004 best-seller now published in 29 languages. It won, among others, the Prix Litteraraire Zepter for European Novel of the Year, France's Prix Millepages, Italy's Premio Acerbi and the Nielsen-Bookscan Golden Book Award. He has also written short stories, film scripts, three stageplays, a biography of the poet Charles Donnelly, and the 'Irish Male' trilogy of comic journalism.